ABOUT THIS BOOK

Welcome to the darker, sexier side of Havenwood Falls that many residents never speak of publicly, but most likely enjoy in secret. Venture into the SIN MC, the VIP rooms of Silk nightclub, and behind other closed doors, where you'll discover passion, unusual penchants, and just how far some will go for love. Hold on to your panties, because it's time to ride . . .

Audrey Smith has never had a place to call home, living as a nomad because of what she is and what she's not. A shifter without a shift, she doesn't belong with a pride, but she's too much "other" to blend in with humans. Her last attempt turned her into a science project. And finding a mate? Forget about it. She'd always been told she wasn't shifter enough for it to happen.

When Audrey totals her car and awakens in Havenwood Falls, she immediately makes plans to leave. But the sexier-than-sin paramedic who pulled her from the wreckage has other ideas, claiming her as his. But based on everything she knows, that's impossible.

Nicholas Jordan never expected to find his mate and settle down. If she lived in Havenwood Falls, he would have met her already. Then Audrey literally crashes into his life. Not only does he want her, but he *needs* her. She belongs to him, and he to her.

Accepting Nicholas's claim would betray everything Audrey's ever believed about herself. But the longer she denies the mating bond, the more dangerous it becomes for them both, putting their lives—and the pride's future—at risk.

HAVENWOOD FALLS SIN & SILK BOOKS

Taming the Beast by Nadirah Foxx

Plans Laid Bare by JD Nelson

Shift of Fate by Victoria Escobar

Stolen Wishes by Victoria Flynn

Damned Allure by Justine Winter

Savage Salvation by Kristie Cook

Dark Seduction by Michele G. Miller & R.K. Ryals

Soul Laid Bare by JD Nelson

Stray With Me by E.J. Fechenda

Chase the Flames by Desiree Lafawn

Flirting With Death by Nadirah Foxx

Also try the signature line, Havenwood Falls, the historical paranormal line, Legends of Havenwood Falls, and stories from the local supernatural college in Sun & Moon Academy.

Stay up to date at www.HavenwoodFalls.com

SHIFT OF FATE

A HAVENWOOD FALLS SIN & SILK NOVELLA

VICTORIA ESCOBAR

CHAPTER 1

AUDREY

The Challenger roared down the winding highway of Colorado. The gas light wasn't on yet, but the time of reckoning would soon be at hand. Skipping a break in the last town proved to be a worse idea with each dark, sign-less mile.

"Audrey, you're a fucking idiot." If I had more sense, I'd turn the car around before there was no chance of making it back. Something visceral possessed me to keep going farther, faster, without stopping. All roads went somewhere, after all—even the dark, empty ones.

When the night terrors returned two days ago, I packed everything I owned—which wasn't much—and left Iowa. The longer the delay, the more the terrors would seep into daily life, and paranoia would eat at my sanity. Been there, done that, and it wasn't pretty or pleasant to think I was crazy.

So I left and drove. Hopefully far enough to leave the terrors behind. For a time. The cycle would eventually start anew, but for a while, I hoped for a pretense of peace.

Stopping would be required soon, though. A body, even one with perks like mine, needed rest and real food to survive. If I went another twenty-four hours without sleep, I might drive my junkyard rescue right off the edge of one of these winding roads. A few years ago, that wouldn't have sounded as scary as it did now.

I leaned over the steering wheel and squinted into the distance. The moonless sky made the dark wilderness somehow darker. The clouds covering the starlight added depth to the darkness, making it appear more like the pit of some abyss than a night-shrouded forest.

There had to be something out here. A homestead, or a cabin. A ski lodge even. I could pay for a room, and maybe talk to someone about gasoline. Even pay to use someone's spare gas can. Anything was better than ending up empty on the side of the road in the middle of nowhere. Especially since I wasn't sure where the road went.

Trees vanished into the horizon all around without showing any promise of civilization. Not even a dirt road that could lead to some recluse's cabin. I loved the wild, but the civilized part of me needed indoor plumbing and hot water heaters. The very thought of a warm bath made my tired eyes flutter closed.

The sudden blast of a new song on the radio jolted me upright. I shook my head and reached for the window to let in some of the cold air. Maybe the icy November chill would keep me awake long enough to reach some kind of destination.

Movement drew my attention back to the road.

"Fuck." I had enough time to register the ghostly looking deer in the road before I hit it and the car spun crazily out of control.

Metal ground against metal, and the noise terrified me. The air bag didn't go off as I threw my hands up to protect my face from the flying glass of the shattered windshield. When the vehicle pinged off the guard rail, my head smashed into the steering wheel. I saw stars in a very literal sense. In seconds, the car came to a sudden, neck-breaking halt in the middle of the road.

My normally crisp vision blurred and spotted; no amount of blinking cleared it. I could smell blood, oil, and gasoline. I tried moving, only to bite my lip against a scream when pain flared throughout my body. Until rescue came, I was stuck. I prayed the car wasn't on fire somewhere.

Would someone come by and see, or would I die on the unnamed road? I closed my eyes and hoped for rescue but waited for death.

~

NICHOLAS

I was only in bed for twenty minutes when the message came through about a car accident on the very edge of the town's border. Instead of bitching about the ungodly hour, I climbed out of bed, dressed, and went out to do my job, calling Liam Peters on the way.

The city was either too cheap or too poor to hire on additional EMTs, but I never questioned it. Job security and all. Liam was a volunteer firefighter with an EMT certification, which made him more valuable than most of the others that took shifts with me. He met me at the ambulance bay of the fire station, wearing his usual sunglasses and carrying coffee.

My jaw cracked as I stifled a yawn. Since getting the paramedic certification a couple of months ago, I'd been busier. There was something nice about being the only certified paramedic in town, but at the same time, it fucked with sleep and anything else normal. I hoped a couple of the graduating high school kids would take the request for EMTs seriously, but I wasn't holding my breath.

If I was lucky, there wouldn't be much to do, the car's occupants would be dead, and I'd get another few hours of sleep before heading to the gym. Since my best friend Braden McCabe died, I made sure to hit the gym at least once a day. I wasn't an alpha, but I'd be damned if I would ever be too weak to save a friend's life again.

"That doesn't look pretty." Liam leaned forward in the seat.

I shifted the ambulance a little so I could see around the slowing tow truck. A whistle cut the air as I got a glimpse of the mangled car. "Elk, you think?"

Liam cocked his head. "Possibly. Only other thing I can think of that damn big is a bear."

My hand ran through my long fringe of hair, which reminded me —I needed a cut. Another thing to add to my list of shit to do when I found time. "Let's see if anyone's alive."

I pulled the ambulance off to the shoulder and climbed out, zipping up my blue work jacket with the bright silver reflective EMS on the back and "JORDAN" written across the left breast. I grabbed the medic box before slamming the door and heading over to the crash.

Shame about the car. The classic, while needing a paint job, was still a dream car for most. Probably some crazy-ass wannabe street racer. Stupid too, to be racing down the county road in the middle of the damn night.

Deputy Conall stood next to the driver's side—what was left of it —while Sheriff Ric Kasun leaned in through the crushed windshield. Conall directed a flashlight in through the mangled windshield. Even with the poor light of not quite dawn, both shifter men should have been able to see fine, but as a cat shifter, I didn't question them and risk a pissing match.

"Liam, Nicholas." Ric pulled his broad body out of the crash. "The girl's breathing, but I can't tell you the extent of the injuries. Joshua." Ric moved away from the crash to have a few words with the mechanic, who already had the tow truck in place.

"Should have brought a metalworker," I muttered, as Liam tried to find a delicate way of reaching the driver. I stepped up to the driver's window, but thanks to the collapsed pillar, I could barely get a hand in. I glanced across and then stood up to look at the other side. "Passenger side looks relatively undamaged."

Liam went around to the other side. He glanced at me as he tried the handle. "Door's locked."

I lifted a brow.

He shrugged and stuck his elbow through the window. "Door's open."

Liam slid into the passenger seat, not even bothered by the newly broken glass. He placed a hand on the girl's head and looked down at the pedals. "Wheel well is collapsed. Looks like her leg could be stuck. She's flirting with death."

"Let's see about getting her out and to the med center."

Liam climbed out of the car. "You're smaller than I am. You get in there and pull her out."

I snorted. "By what, two inches?"

"Wide, ass wipe. Despite your gym hours, you're still scrawny."

"Like fucking hell I am." But I moved into position and slid into the car. "Get the damn stretcher."

Her seatbelt was still firmly in place and the first thing I had to deal with. At least the girl was smart enough to be wearing it. Too often I got called out and the seatbelt hadn't been able to do its job.

I angled her so she would fall against my chest when I cut the strap. My safety tool sliced the belt like cutting butter. Her weight didn't even register when she tipped, and it brought a frown to my face. For her height—she was nearly as tall as me—she was too light.

With her face tilted toward the light, I could see sharp angles in her cheeks and a pallor to her skin that shouted malnutrition. My fingers ghosted over her cheek, careful of the bruises. Her lashes fluttered, and for a frozen moment in time, her molten gold gaze stared into my eyes.

Mine.

The unexpected claim slammed into me as hard as the elk had her car. All my muscles tensed. I fought a small battle with myself to stay calm and not lose my damn mind. She was injured, for fuck's sake.

The damn cat inside me took notice, and I forced my gaze away, closing my eyes. There was a time and a place—and this sure as hell wasn't it.

"Jordan, what's taking so long?" Liam tapped the hood next to my head. His head tipped just enough to let me know he noticed. The hellhound was perceptive as fuck.

"Yeah, yeah." I shifted under his scrutiny and returned my attention to where the woman's feet should be. She whimpered a bit when I tried to pull her free, but didn't regain consciousness. "Her left foot is stuck, and she's bleeding from her right leg. By the bruising, she's likely concussed as well."

"Let me get some help over here." Liam stepped away and flagged down Ric and Joshua.

I took a chance and glanced down at the woman again, but this time her eyes were closed. Dried blood crusted along her golden hairline and marred her temple. Her shoulder looked out of place . . . but she did otherwise look in one piece. My major concern now was getting her—my mate—out of the vehicle. Fate had a fucking twisted sense of humor.

CHAPTER 2

AUDREY

*P*ain entered my consciousness before anything else. Everything hurt. No amount of subtle shifting relieved it.

When I forced my eyes open, the ceiling above my head didn't have the familiar pattern of water stains in my room. I flailed into an upright position, with my heart pounding in my ears before the memory of the accident came back. I wasn't in Iowa anymore.

I rolled a shoulder and winced at the pain that radiated down to my fingertips. Motion from the left caught my eye. I froze.

An old man sat in a chair positioned in front of a curtain, with a book in hand. His eyes reminded me of ice storms in Montana, and I waited as their frosty blue gaze studied me. "Finally awake."

"How long have I been out?" I noted my back and neck hurt almost as much as my shoulder when I shifted in his direction. I racked my memory, trying to put the pieces back together.

I was nearly sure he wasn't the man who pulled me out of my car. He was too old to be doing rescue work, even though the intensity of his stare spoke volumes of his authority. The cane leaning against his chair added to the elderly visage.

"If you passed out immediately after the accident, then around sixteen hours. With the bump on your head, no one was sure if or when you would wake up." He stood, sliding the book into his pocket and grabbing his cane. "I'm Elsmed Fairchild. Welcome to Havenwood Falls."

"Havenwood Falls? I'm still in Colorado, right?" I rolled my pained shoulder a second time and grimaced as the bite went deep.

"You are. Where are you from?" He stepped up to the side of the bed, and I did my best to avoid his deep, soul-burning gaze.

"I'm driving from Iowa. Or I was." I grimaced as I attempted to find a comfortable sitting position. "I haven't hurt this bad in a while."

"You're lucky you're alive, really. Mule deer wouldn't have caused that kind of damage. The sheriff is assuming it's an elk, though no one has come forward with the kill. What was in Iowa, if I may ask?"

"Nothing important enough to keep me there." Giving up, I flopped back in the bed and closed my eyes. I wish I had something to deal with the deep aching.

"I'll call the nurse in and get you something for the pain in a moment."

I didn't voice how creepy it was he seemed to have read my mind. "Do you sit in on all accident patients who are unconscious?"

"Only the supernatural ones."

My eyes shot open and darted to his face. "Mr. Fairchild, I'm not supernatural."

The denial was automatic. I didn't pretend to not know what he talked about. There was something preternatural about his demeanor that said he wouldn't take bullshit. Even as old as he was.

"Yet you're not denying they exist, as most normal humans would. Your shift is there in your mind, but her presence is faint, almost as if she is covered, or blocked somehow." Mr. Fairchild shook his head. "It's not something that needs immediate attention."

I shifted, uncomfortable with the topic, as I always was when someone asked about it. "When can I leave?"

"Dr. Underwood mentioned something about a concussion. Now that you're awake, they'll likely be able to address that. Probably some kind of observation."

"Oh."

"I haven't left Havenwood Falls in some years. Tell me, do they talk about the Collector outside our little canyon?"

"Collector of what? There are all sorts of collectors in Denver. I met a dragon in Chicago that liked to collect shifter pelts. I didn't stay there long. Do you know what happened to my car?"

Mr. Fairchild pursed his lips a moment before speaking. "Joshua runs the tow company for Havenwood Falls. You'll want to talk to him, most likely."

"Oh, okay." I closed my eyes again, suddenly swamped by a wave of fatigue.

"I must inform you, there are rules for supernaturals here. I'm sure you'll understand in time. Due to current events in town, you'll need to be registered before you can leave the medical center. For your safety as much as the town's. Adelaide will come and discuss all that with you tomorrow."

Registered? I fought to stay awake enough to process the words. "But I don't have a shift."

"Knowledge is power, Ms. Smith. Never forget that. I'll fetch a nurse for you."

"Thank you." I clenched my jaw to keep from yawning. The voices outside the curtain faded into a dull murmur that reminded me of a stream's trickle as I drifted between wakefulness and sleep.

My mind lingered on Elsmed Fairchild a moment. What a strange individual. He felt powerful without looking it. As I drifted off to sleep, I realized he had said my name without me giving it to him. What kind of town was Havenwood Falls?

NICHOLAS

My parents have always been the rock in the storm of my life. Whenever I needed help—whether it be physical, like replacing the roof on my cabin, or emotional, dealing with the grief of Braden's passing—they were there. They made it clear when I was a child they would always have my back, and they had never let me down.

The drive through Creekwood wasn't long enough to put my thoughts in order. Tension followed me from the day before, and I hoped they'd provide a solution. My parents had always hoped I'd settle down with a nice local girl, regardless of supernatural status. A stranger from out of town, whose name I didn't even know, wasn't what I'd been expecting. Not that I really had been expecting anything at all. I enjoyed my bachelor life, and at thirty, still had plenty of years ahead of me to settle down.

I didn't knock on the door of my childhood home. If my parents weren't home, I'd have to say something to them about the fact I didn't have to use my key to get in. Despite crime being relatively low, there was no point in encouraging the temptation.

The familiarity of the house washed over me when I stepped in, but did nothing to relieve my tension. "Mom? Dad?"

"In the office, honey."

I followed Mom's shout to the office, where I found both my parents. Dad sat behind the desk, and Mom sat in the lounge chair thing by the bookcase. A book lay in Mom's lap; she liked Dad's company even if they didn't say a word to each other.

I pulled out the leather chair and sat down in it, but immediately stood and paced. There was no way I could sit at a time like this.

"Shouldn't my favorite son be at work?" Mom grinned and winked.

"I could say the same of my mother. My reports are caught up, and the station is clean." I rolled my shoulders, suddenly uncomfortable with the topic I wanted to bring up. "I didn't come to talk about work."

Mom canted her head. "Hoping for an easy meal? You're welcome to come for dinner tonight."

"It's not that either, though I appreciate the offer."

Dad looked away from his monitor and at me. "What do you need, Nicholas?"

My hand ran over my still-too-long hair. I'd stop at the barber after this. "I've met my mate—I think."

Mom sat up. "You think?"

Dad folded his hands in the *don't bullshit a bullshitter* pose of my youth. "Mates either are or aren't, son. There's no in between."

"I know that. You don't think I know that?" I walked over to the liquor cabinet in the corner and looked for something to pour.

"It's a little early—" Dad cut off.

"What happened, Nicholas?" Mom's voice was soft as I poured a scotch.

I tossed it back before answering her. "I had a rescue yesterday morning. Car accident. And don't start about the falling in love with the rescued shit. I took the classes. I know the deal. Why do you think I waited a day?" I poured another drink. The scotch wouldn't get me drunk—at least, not for long. Now if I tapped into Dad's bottle of Fey Spirits . . ."

"So you went on a rescue?" Dad leaned back in his chair.

"Ten seconds, maybe. I had ten seconds of eye contact." The second drink went down as smoothly as the first. I faced my parents. "How did you know? That you belonged to each other?"

"It's visceral, Nicholas. Tell us how you feel." Mom set her book aside.

"Tense. There's an energy I can't burn off, and I've tried. Restless, anxious, unsettled." I began pacing again. "There's no reason to be this way. I don't even know the girl's name."

"What's stopping you from finding out?" Dad's eyes followed my movement.

"She's unconscious. Or was, when I took her in. I lingered when Dr. Underwood went in to look at her. Concussion. Dislocated shoulder. Fractured two ribs—where the seatbelt held her in place. Sprained ankle that would heal faster if it was actually broken instead. Honestly, she's damn lucky to be alive."

"Is she a shifter?" Mom asked.

I shrugged. "Smelled like a cat. Couldn't tell you what kind." I shoved both my hands in my hair and pulled. "I feel like I should be doing something, but don't know what that is. There's this . . . thing. It feels like it's pushing, but I have no fucking idea where or why."

"Start small." Dad gestured to the door. "You know she's unconscious, but was in a car accident. Do the things she can't do for herself at the moment. Where are her things? Has the insurance been contacted?"

"Does she have toiletries and items to clean up with when she wakes up?" Mom added.

"What's that supposed to do?" I stared at them both. They'd lost their minds. How were menial tasks supposed to identify this girl as a mate?

"It gives you time to figure out what you feel, and gives you vague insight to her life before the accident." Mom gave me a pointed look. "Only you can determine if this girl is your mate or not. If she is, you'll know."

"How? That's what I came to you for. How will I know? How did you know?" I glared from one to the other. "You're not going to help at all?"

Dad sighed. "We are helping, but we're not going to hold your hand through it. You're a grown, respectable man, and I couldn't ask for a finer son. However, if you can't figure out the basics of a mate, then somewhere along the line, I failed as a father."

"You haven't failed, Dad. I just . . ."

"It's scary and new." Mom stood and wrapped me in a hug. "You've always been so sure, and then when Braden died, you used your grief to become the best man you can be. But you never questioned the path you walked. Now you're uncertain. Flailing in the unknown. Take our advice. Go, do for her what she can't do for herself. And go visit Rose at Howe's. Ask her for the soaps and such that I get from her. A shifter woman would appreciate the gently scented items."

I sighed and hugged Mom back. "I don't want to go about this the wrong way."

"You can only be who you are, Nicholas. Trust in fate." She kissed my cheek and pulled away. "Shoo. Your father has paperwork to finish."

"Thanks." The dismissal stung, especially when it felt like they hadn't provided any information at all, but I did as asked. They wouldn't provide anything else even if I camped in the office with them.

The only thing I could do was follow instructions. Joshua towed the car; he likely had all her things. As far as starting points went, it was better than anything else I could think of. Since Howe's was around the corner from the garage, it wouldn't hurt to stop there too.

CHAPTER 3

AUDREY

a big man in comfortable-looking flannel and kind silvery eyes was the first to appear in the morning. Well, after the nurses woke me for the millionth time to ask my name and date of birth. He dragged the chair over to the side of the bed and sat. This close to me, I could smell his wolf.

"I'm Sheriff Ric Kasun. How are you feeling?" He pulled out a tiny notebook from the front pocket of his flannel, along with an equally tiny pen.

"I'd be better if they'd have let me sleep through the night." I stretched my arms over my head and winced when my shoulder pulled. The damn thing was going to take forever to heal.

"I've begun to write out the police report." Ric flipped open his notebook. "You were out of it when we arrived on the scene, but it's clear you hit an elk. I still need your statement for the report."

I chewed on my lip and debated a lie. In the end, his supernatural attributes decided for me. I skirted around the fact I might have fallen asleep behind the wheel, but kept the story mostly intact.

"Ghostly?" Ric scribbled on his police pad. "Magical is a possibility then, but you did say you were extremely tired. Though it does explain why no one in the community has found the elk yet. An animal that size isn't easily hidden."

Before I could reply, a woman colorfully dressed somewhere between boho and rocker chic entered the little room. An old leather messenger bag threatened to fall off her shoulder. "Oh, good, you're still awake. Taylor said you might be back asleep. Healing takes a toll on the body. I'm Addie. I'll be your tattoo artist today."

"Audrey." I frowned. "Tattoo?"

"For the Registry. We track supernaturals to monitor misuse of power and to assist in preventing the laws from being broken. Visitors get a temporary one, and residents have a permanent one." Addie sat on the edge of the bed. She rifled through her bag and pulled out a small notepad. "So what do you want for your design?"

"But I don't have a shift." I looked between the two.

The sheriff crossed his arms. "Being a shifter is a . . . complicated thing. You *could* be diluted too far to shift or you could have suffered a trauma that prevents you from shifting or . . . there are a lot of other reasons, and there's no point going over all of them. The point is, you do have shifter in you, and enough supernatural qualities to warrant being in the Registry."

"I agree." Addie tapped her pencil against the notebook. "It'll be temporary, anyway, since you'll need to get your car situated and you don't even know if you like Havenwood Falls yet. We can reevaluate after you figure out what you want to do."

"I've never thought about a tattoo." I chewed on my lower lip.

"Think about the things you like. Your personality or beliefs." Addie stared, waiting.

I sighed and stared out past Addie and Ric. "I have really bad nightmares sometimes. It's the only consistent part of my life. Unless you count the traveling. I move around quite a bit. I don't have any real beliefs. I loved bartending in Vegas. Los Angeles was beautiful."

Addie's pencil hurried over her paper. In a few minutes, she turned it around for me to see—a simple dream catcher, with a few extra lines and an arrow to create a compass out of the same circle. A skeleton key hung on the southeast side of the compass, and a horseshoe hung on the southwest side.

"It's beautiful." I looked beyond the image to Addie. "You're very talented."

"Thank you. Where do you want it, and we'll get it transferred?" Addie stood up from the chair.

I looked down at myself and shifted muscles gently to find the least painful place. I held out my right arm and tapped the spot right below the inside of my elbow. "I think this is the only unbruised part of me."

"Fair enough." Addie pulled a small tattoo machine from the bag.

I frowned. "I didn't know they made portable tattoo machines."

Addie winked. "We have our ways in Havenwood Falls."

Ric tapped his pen against the notebook. "Addie, have you heard anything about dark spells a couple nights ago?"

Addie shook her head as she took my arm and began the tattooing process. "No, why?"

"Audrey mentioned the elk looked ghostly. I thought a spell may have gone awry, or the wards."

I closed my eyes as the tattoo machine began to buzz. There was a reason I never thought about a tattoo. My stomach clenched a little, and I forced some calm, even breaths out.

Addie snorted. "That's not how the wards are built to work. They don't manifest into physical forms."

"Still, it's worth having someone look at the car. Maybe it's that curse you mentioned reacting with the wards. Bishop would be able to pick up any magic residue on her car, right? Roman said he wanted to be informed of unusual activity." Ric scribbled some more notes.

"Roman's been harder to deal with than normal recently. If you give me some time to check on my appointments, I'll go with you instead of bothering him." Addie set the tattoo machine aside and pulled out some other supplies from her bag with one hand.

"I have what I need for the report. I'll get that to you as soon as I can. Where will you be staying, Audrey?" The sheriff slipped his notebook away.

I flinched a little as the numbness from the constant sting faded away to actual pain. "I don't know where I'll be staying yet. I have to talk to whoever towed my car, and get my things."

"I can talk to Michaela, and we can reserve you a room at the inn. I can run you down to the garage when you're released, then take you to the inn. It's the best place until you can figure out your next step. I'll leave my card with my number, so you can call when you know when you can leave." Addie unfolded a cloth and dabbed lightly at the tattoo.

"Thank you." I didn't have the energy to question why she was being so helpful and just took it as part of her nature. Some people were like that, and had to help.

"You're welcome." Addie nodded, but her eyes were on my arm, where she wiped over the tattoo.

I followed her gaze and watched as the ink wiped away as if she'd drawn the tattoo with a ballpoint. "Is that supposed to happen?"

The other woman shook her head. "No. It's never happened before."

"What is it?" Ric stepped forward and watched Addie clean away the rest of the ink.

Addie's fingers probed the spot she'd tried to ink. Something intangible rippled in the air and made the hairs on my neck stand up. "There's something blocking the Registry. It feels malevolent. It wouldn't be wise to poke at it further without a full circle."

I tried to wrap my head around what Addie was saying. "I'm . . . cursed?"

"In layman's terms . . . yes, I suppose calling it a curse is the best term. It could be a geis or seal as well, but curse works. At a guess, based on what you've told us and the energy it throws out, I'd say it prevents your shift, and might have something to do with your nightmares, too. There's no way to know for certain without taking it apart, though, and that's never a good idea without knowing the who and why."

"Is she a danger to Havenwood Falls?" Ric squared up his shoulders and looked ready to haul me out of bed and drag me outside.

"No." Addie took my cold hand in hers. "We'll have to come up with something else for the Registry. If I'm right, I can charm a bracelet or necklace, and you can wear that. The curse—let's call it that for now—might apply to anything attempting to touch you directly. I wish I could examine it more, but it's not safe to mess with it without a circle and quite possibly a full moon. The moon was full at Thanksgiving. We'll have to wait for December's moon to poke at it."

"That's . . . You've given me more than anyone else has. I've never considered I might be magically cursed. I mean, as a child growing up in the foster system, I considered myself unlucky or cursed, but never like this. It's ironic in a way."

Addie cleaned up her supplies. "Foster care?"

I lay back down in the bed and closed my eyes. "Yes. A couple of boaters found me floating in the Rappahannock River in Virginia when I was eleven. I have no memory of anything before waking in the hospital. No one came to claim me."

"I'm sorry. That had to be hard." She patted my arm. "Well, you're here now, and Havenwood Falls has a way of making everyone feel at home."

Ric stood and moved to the entry. "I think I heard something about keeping you overnight again to monitor your concussion. They'll likely let you go in the morning, when they've determined you're okay enough to not need watching."

"Give me a call when they tell you if they're going to discharge you." Addie stood and followed the sheriff. "Welcome to Havenwood Falls, Audrey."

"See you in the morning." I clenched my jaw to keep from yawning, but could do nothing to keep fatigue from dropping me into unconsciousness. For the first time in days, I rested peacefully.

CHAPTER 4

AUDREY

*T*he nurse's lecture went in one ear and out the other as I carefully changed into the simple button-down shirt and jeans Addie brought. My body still hurt—the shirt was a bitch to get on with my shoulder—and there was a deep ache in my soul I didn't understand, but overall, I was in one piece and didn't need to remain in the medical center.

"Thanks." I took the offered paperwork from the nurse and skimmed it. The instructions were basic common sense, and the billing information was listed at the bottom. I hoped the car insurance would cover most of it—if not all. I'd have to stay in Havenwood Falls a lot longer if there was a medical bill to pay as well as buy a new car. I didn't like to leave a place with debt to chase me.

"You really should allow the doctor to splint or boot your foot. It will heal faster with less stress." The nurse shifted to stay in my line of vision as I turned to Addie.

I shook my head at her. "I've allowed the doctor the compression sleeve, and I've promised to rest often and follow the instructions. It's good enough."

She wrung her hands together, but stepped aside. "At least the cane or crutches for assistance with rest?"

With a wave of my hand, I said my goodbye and hurried behind Addie.

"Oh. Before I forget." Addie dug around in her pocket as she led the way out of the medical center. She pulled out a pendant and tossed it.

I caught the necklace with one hand, the green striped stone pendant swinging like a pendulum. I frowned at it, then at Addie.

"It's for the Registry." Addie stopped outside the door and waited for me to follow. "Let's see if this works."

I pulled the long chain up over my head. The teardrop stone felt warm against my skin, but nothing happened that I could tell.

Addie's smile proved something different. "It works. Come on. The stone is malachite, in case you're wondering. Don't take it off for any reason. It's waterproof."

"What's malachite?" I limped after Addie, wishing I had accepted the cane, to a well-kept Jeep.

"A protection stone, for the most part. Helps with creativity and intuition, and wards against nightmares." Addie nodded at my surprise. "Seemed like something you would appreciate."

"Thanks. Does it actually work?" I climbed up and buckled in as Addie started the engine.

Her grin held mischief. "Let me know."

Addie pointed out some of the landmarks as she drove. The town looked like Christmastown relocated to Havenwood Falls for the holidays. Miller's Plaza held a bunch of interesting shops, and their decorations looked like they were trying to one-up each other.

Addie turned onto Eighth Street and then pulled into a lot behind a garage. "I'm going to have to leave you here. I have some errands to run, but the inn is right on Main Street. Just go back up and walk down past the shops. You can't miss it."

"Thanks, Addie. For all your help." I hopped out of the Jeep and winced as I came down too hard on my ankle. As I approached the garage, Addie tooted the horn, making me jump, and my ankle screamed its protest when I pivoted to look back.

Addie's head was out her window. "Ask for Joshua."

I gave her a thumbs up and tried not to limp walking into the little office. No one sat at the reception desk, and no one sat in any of the plastic waiting chairs. I hesitated, unsure of what to do, when a door leading to the garage's bays swung open and a man stepped through.

He cocked his head while he wiped his hands on a towel. His gray hair nearly matched his eyes. "Help you?"

"I'm here to speak to Joshua about my car." My hands white-knuckled around my purse strap. The car was my everything, and now . . .

"I'm Joshua. You'd be the Challenger girl, then." He stuffed the cloth in a back pocket before holding open the garage door. "Shall we take a look?"

Tears blurred my vision when I got a good look at what remained of my car. I should have been grateful I was alive and the car took the brunt of the damage, but I loved that car. I took a deep breath and put a choke hold on my emotions. It was only a car, and it was decades old. It could probably be fixed. Most anything could nowadays.

"You're a lucky one." Joshua tapped on the crumpled driver's side with a fist. "It's going to cost more time and money to fix than you probably originally paid for it."

I could only nod as his words sunk in. By the sound of it, I couldn't afford to fix it even if I wanted to. "The sheriff said he was writing the report, and I've got to get this reported to the insurance company."

"Nick was in here yesterday, and pulled your insurance information from the glove box. I let him use my office to get that started for you."

"Oh." I didn't know a Nick, but felt it wasn't polite to say so. "I have stuff in the trunk."

"He insisted we pull it out for you. It's locked in the office. He's probably right—it's not wise to let it sit in the garage. Not that I don't trust my boys, but there's less temptation that way. The devil's a cagey bastard."

"Thank you. Is there a junkyard around that I can sell the car to, or do you take care of that? I've never wrecked a car before." I followed Joshua back through the reception and into his office.

My things were stacked in a neat pile in the corner. The old-fashioned trunk held clothes, while the actual suitcase held shoes. A messenger bag sat on top with all of my electronics, and my book bag with overnight necessities rested against the suitcase. Overall, it was a pitiful number of items to sum up my life.

"Have a seat, dear. Can I get you anything? A drink?" Joshua sighed as he lowered himself into his office chair when I shook my head. "There's not much you can do about the car just yet. An insurance adjuster will likely want to come and take a look, though I can tell you right off, there's no way they're going to do anything more than call it totaled."

"Okay." My knees gave out, and I sank into the guest chair. The small hope of getting it fixed went out the window.

"You'll want to talk to Nick, and see how far he's gotten with reporting it to your insurance, and check their timeline. Havenwood Falls is off the beaten path, so getting any kind of payout is going to take time."

I nodded again. I was losing the battle with my emotions, and a traitorous tear trickled out of my left eye.

Joshua pushed a box of tissues in my direction. "You're allowed to cry. If I totaled a car like yours, I'd cry too. If you'd like, I can estimate its worth—what the insurance will likely pay—and we can discuss what you'd like to do about transportation."

"Okay." I sniffled into a tissue and wiped at my eyes. Taking a steadying breath, I met Joshua's patient gaze. "I'm sorry. I really appreciate your help."

He waved off the apology. "I have an auction coming up. What are you looking for in a car? I doubt we can get the same one."

"I picked that one because it's safe, and easy enough for me to maintain myself." My hand fisted around the tissue, and he nudged the wastebasket over with his foot.

"You know cars?" Joshua's brows rose.

My left shoulder rose and fell. "Enough to change the oil, rotate the tires, top off the fluids, change the brake pads, spark plugs . . . easy simple stuff really, but it all costs money to do if I took it to a garage."

"Sure does." Joshua leaned back in his chair and scribbled some notes on a nearby pad. "Anything else? Color, preferred make or model?"

"Cheaper parts would be nice. Parts for the Challenger aren't cheap."

"No. They're not." Joshua's pencil scratched across the paper. "I think Honda. They've got a good inexpensive line. And they run forever with the right care. I noticed the Challenger was a clutch. Still want a manual?"

"I don't know how much the insurance will pay out." I chewed on my lip. "Whatever's affordable, I guess."

"Don't worry about that right now. You tend to those bruises and sores. Health comes first. We can make arrangements if you don't get a fair deal."

"All right." I took a breath. "Okay. What do I have to do?"

∾

NICHOLAS

I JOGGED up the short flight of steps to the medical center with a plain white gift bag in one hand. After spending the day before at the garage with Audrey's totaled car and her scent fogging my brain, I figured the best course of action—for both of us—was to be straightforward. Tell her what I thought; ask her how she felt. Kiss her stupid and go from there.

With the mountain lion population split between two families in Havenwood Falls, I thought I had more time to find "the one" and settle down. I thought it would happen when I was in Denver certifying, or renewing, but fate decided to play her hand. I either went with it or died from it. I wasn't really ready for either, but the choices were limited.

I nodded to the nurse at the desk. She smiled, and with my focus on Audrey, I couldn't remember her name.

"Hey, handsome. Whatcha up to?" The interest in her gaze might have drawn my attention once, but not any longer.

My cat bristled, wanting to ignore her and go find our mate. I quelled the cat and kept my smile friendly. The human wouldn't understand the blowoff, and I had to work with her. "Figured the car wreck girl would like some provisions. We didn't exactly grab anything from her car but her."

The nurse fluttered over her station. "Aren't you sweet? She discharged about an hour ago, though. Left with Addie. Refused the boot or splint. She's only going to injure herself further. I can take that bag off your hands if you want. I'm sure some other injured soul would appreciate it just as much."

I stepped back as my mind spun. Checked out? Where would she go? And why did she refuse medical care? "I didn't think she'd be leaving so soon, with her injuries, but I'm not a doctor."

"Dr. Underwood gave the okay." The nurse cocked her head, still smiling. As a predator, I recognized that smile, and stepped back a couple more paces as she came around the desk.

"Thanks. I appreciate it." I hurried out the way I came in before the nurse got any closer, and tossed the gift bag across the truck in frustration when I climbed back in. Where would a girl from nowhere go, if she had no vehicle to get her there? To the garage. To check on said vehicle, and likely gather her things.

I threw the truck in gear and pulled out onto Main Street in a hurry. Despite Havenwood Falls being a small town, there were times I didn't cross paths with my own family unless I wanted to. If I missed her at the garage, there was no telling when I'd find her again.

The light at Eighth forced me to stop—the driver in front of me didn't give me enough room to turn—and I idly noted that Leda had changed the jewelry display again at Summit Jewelers. The Christmas display highlighted several very classy and expensive-looking pieces. Would Audrey want a pretty ring to show off, as most women did? Was my mate more human than shifter, or vice versa? I'd have to ask.

As I drummed my fingers on my steering wheel with impatience, my eyes landed on a figure walking up the block. I narrowed my eyes and cursed. I may have only seen and held her once, but I knew in my gut the figure limping up the street was Audrey.

She shouldn't even be out of the med center, let alone dragging a trunk and loaded down with her baggage. I'd have to have a word with Underwood. A concussion along with all the other slew of damages—especially the ribs—warranted more than one day of medical attention.

Why the hell hadn't anyone offered to help her?

When the light turned green, I launched the truck up the street, squealing the tires, and pulled into the closest spot to my mate. I remembered to shut the truck off as I jumped out. Ric would have my head for unreasonable idling—our mountain air was pristine and we liked to keep it that way. I marched up to her with no clear idea of what to say.

My anger grew as I noticed she had a suitcase bungee-corded to the antique trunk, and wore a backpack and messenger bag. The words flew out before I considered them. "What the fuck do you think you're doing?"

She jolted, and when her golden eyes landed on my face, the force of the bond stole the air from my lungs. She sucked in a sharp breath, her eyes widening. I watched what little color she had drain from her face.

"It's not possible." Her words were almost lost to the noise of the traffic, but I caught them.

What wasn't possible? Didn't matter. We could have that conversation later.

"Get in the truck." I yanked the trunk handle out of her hand and walked toward my vehicle, expecting her to follow.

"I don't even know who the hell you are. Why would I get into a vehicle with you?" She grabbed for her case, but I pulled it out of reach.

The fact she wasn't a mouse amused and impressed me. When she glared, clearly ready for a fight, I struggled not to laugh. I liked a woman with spunk, and she appeared to have plenty.

"Nicholas Jordan. The guy who pulled you out of your mangled vehicle." I resisted the urge to touch her, stroke a finger down her cheek or wrap an arm around her. I *needed* to touch her, the way a starving man needed food, but if I did so, I wouldn't stop, and there were laws about allowable public activities.

She didn't seem the least bit impressed as she crossed her arms, drawing my attention to the puckered tips of her breasts. I wasn't the only horny one on the sidewalk. "Thanks, I guess. Give me my trunk."

I tossed the trunk and suitcase into the truck bed behind me with an easy fling. "Listen, kitten. I'm not having this conversation out on the street."

She snarled, but it only excited my cat. "I have nothing I want to talk to you about. The med center has my insurance. You'll get paid."

I leaned toward her and watched with fascination as her pupils dilated. Her breaths quickened, and I craved to close the remaining distance and seal my mouth over hers. I'd give her a real reason to gasp . . . but not in front of Coffee Haven. Not where all the old biddies could see, and gossip about it.

"No." Her breath tickled my mouth when I closed the distance to less than a hair's breadth, with the implication of a kiss. She smelled like the med center, and it wasn't as much of a turnoff as I thought it would be.

"Not here," I corrected. There were a lot more things I wanted besides a kiss, and that wouldn't be appropriate on the street. "Get in the truck, or I put you in the truck."

Tension coursed through the air for a heartbeat before she broke eye contact. "Fine."

She pivoted, and cried out as she crumpled. Before I could think about moving, I held her in my arms, mindful of the broken ribs. If I were any slower, she would have hit the concrete on her bad side. I watched her carefully as I helped her back up.

My fingers moved of their own accord, caressing small patterns on her soft skin, unable to let her go. I nuzzled her hair, unable to resist her allure. "I'm pretty sure the med center gave you a list of things not to do on a sprained ankle, and I think pivoting like you're in the military is on that list."

"Fuck off." She shoved me away and limped toward the passenger door. She pulled her bags off as she approached the door and tossed the book bag in the bed with her trunk.

I wondered if she was just as fiery in bed. The thought made my dick hard, and I couldn't wait to test the theory. Would she scratch and bite? I hoped so.

After counting to ten and taking several deep breaths, I walked around the truck and joined her. With every prolonged moment, my control slipped a little more. The mate bond wasn't meant to be fought, but embraced. Figuratively and literally. How the fuck she was so calm?

"So," I buckled up, mindful of my painful erection, "where to?"

"Whisper Falls Inn. Addie said the rooms would be reasonable even with the season about to start." She didn't look at me, but stared out the window at the shops.

"Do you like coffee? I could run in and get you some?" I suddenly felt awkward and didn't know why.

"Not right now."

I nudged the white bag she'd moved to the center seat. "It's a gift for you."

She eyed the bag with suspicion. "What is it?"

"Take a look." I angled in the seat to watch her study the bag before pulling out a bottle.

Audrey studied the handwritten label before opening the bottle and sniffing. "Soap?"

The light citrus and herb wafted through the truck cab. Mom's floral was too old lady esk in my mind, so I hoped Audrey was okay with the fruity aroma. For a moment, I imagined kissing her skin after bathing and wondered if she'd taste as good as she smelled. "There's shampoo, conditioner, lotion, too. My mother gets them from Rose at Howe's. They're gentler on the senses than the human stuff."

"Thanks, I guess." She dropped the bottle back into the bag.

27

A low growl rumbled in my chest. My job was easier than dealing with Audrey's prickliness. Maybe it was a perverse form of caution. Though I couldn't figure out why. "I have a guest room in my cabin. I wouldn't charge you for its use."

"I don't take handouts." She finally looked at me. "Are you going to drive or should I get out and start walking again?"

"It may take a while to get a replacement for your car." To prolong moving, I checked all the mirrors twice before pulling out into traffic.

"So Joshua told me." She leaned against the door, as far away from me as possible, and it pissed me off.

"Listen." I reached out for her hand, and she slapped me away. "There's no running from this."

She straightened in her seat. "I don't know what you're talking about."

"Bullshit. You're so scared of the bond, you won't even look me in the face." I side-eyed her without taking my attention from the road.

"You're driving, asshole. Your eyes should be on the road, not my face." Her matter-of-fact tone—with not even a hint of anger—made me angrier.

I took a deep breath and tried again. We were stuck, fates chosen, and there was no way around it. If I let her piss me off at every turn, I was going to spend a lot of time angry. "Let's start over. Hi. I'm Nicholas Jordan."

The perverse creature didn't even turn from the window. "Audrey Smith."

"Nice to meet you."

"Sure."

The muscles in my jaw twitched. The tension in the truck was almost suffocating. When I pulled into the inn's lot, Audrey jumped out almost before we completely stopped. I wasn't going to let her ghost me. No way in hell. It wouldn't end well for either of us.

CHAPTER 5

NICHOLAS

I beat Audrey to her bags in the truck bed. Instead of submitting to her silent demand for her bags—like holding her hand out was really going to work—I walked toward the front of the inn.

"Michaela could tell you more, but the inn has been here since the founding of the town." I waited for her at the door and grinned when she tilted her head, as if trying to imagine the old Victorian manor back in the day.

"Why is it Whisper Falls Inn then, instead of Havenwood Falls Inn?"

I tipped my head and focused my hearing. On busy days it was hard, especially now with the ski resort open for the winter season, and people enjoying the brisk fall air, but I could still hear them. I wondered if she could. "Close your eyes and listen."

Skepticism crossed her face before she did as I asked. My stomach twisted when a genuine smile lit her face. I fought the urge to gather her close and kiss her stupid. There would be time for that. I needed to be patient.

"Is that a waterfall?"

"Yes." I couldn't help the gruffness in my voice and was glad my hands were full, or I'd have been all over her when her eyes locked onto mine.

Her smile faded, and the wall between us returned. "I should check in."

I followed her into the inn and waited with her until Sindi came out to the lobby, wiping her hands on a towel. She tucked the edge of it into the back pocket of her impossibly tight pants.

"Hey. Welcome to Whisper Falls Inn." The pretty redheaded vampire tipped her chin at us as she took her place behind the front desk.

"Hi. I'm Audrey. I'm sorry. I don't have a reservation—" Audrey began, but Sindi smiled.

"It's okay. Addie was here yesterday and told Michaela and me all about it. I'm Sindi, by the way. You've had some pretty bad luck the last couple of days. However, Michaela did put one of the rooms upstairs on reserve for you. You have to share a bathroom, but it's a fair price until you get situated."

"Thanks." Audrey set her purse on the desk and rifled around.

"How long will you be staying?" Sindi tapped away at a keyboard.

"Oh, um." Audrey froze. She ticked off something on her fingers and sighed. "Honestly, I don't know."

"Let's start with a week, then. We can always adjust it after you get things figured out."

"That sounds wonderful. Thank you." Audrey pulled out a wallet the size of a small purse. How she couldn't find it in her purse I couldn't figure.

I shifted and drew Sindi's attention. I shook my head and mouthed the word "mate," hoping she'd understand my silent plea. Even without sound to the word, standing this close, her vampire hearing should pick it up—and hopefully not the prickly kitten in front of me. Sindi continued to smile, but I saw a sparkle of curiosity in her gaze that wasn't there before. Whether or not she'd help me out was another matter.

Audrey flipped open the wallet and hesitated over the line of cards before pulling out a gold one. "Use this one."

Sindi tapped away and swiped the card. Frowned and swiped again. "I'm sorry, but it's declining."

I forced my face to remain uninterested when Audrey cut a suspicious look over at me. I smiled at her. "Need some help? I have a guest room, as I mentioned before."

She hissed out a breath and turned her attention back to Sindi. "The card is brand new. It can't have declined. I've never used it."

"Maybe you forgot to activate it." I stepped up before Sindi would have to make up a lie. "Happens, you know. Here." I fished out my wallet and held out my AMEX Platinum card. I never used the damn thing, and since my life was relatively low key, I had decent savings and credit. Jobless and homeless Audrey wouldn't be able to attest to the same. "Put it on mine."

"No." Audrey turned and jabbed a finger into my chest. "You're not paying for my room."

"Two choices, kitten. I pay for your room, so you have a room, since your card declined, or you come stay in my guest room at no cost." I covered her mouth with a hand when she opened it to spew more distaste at me. I shivered when her tongue darted out and licked my palm. It took all my control not to groan. "And I will add these are nonnegotiable choices."

"You can always switch the card later, after you get it straightened out." Sindi shrugged when both of us glared at her. "We don't charge the full price until after checkout anyway."

Audrey shoved me back. "Fine. I'll call the card company later."

Sindi set a key on the desk along with a paper printout. "Last room on the right, closest to the bathroom. Fair warning, it's the noisiest room, but the least expensive."

Audrey grabbed the key and tossed the paper at me. "I've had worse."

Without a word, I followed her up the stairs, wondering what was worse than water pipes and flushing toilets even as my eyes took in her curves from behind.

"Stop looking at my ass." Audrey didn't turn.

"What makes you think I am?" I wondered if I should bring up the fact my guest room had its own bathroom and less noise than the inn would have.

"Because you have a dick in your pants."

I bit my tongue instead of responding. My mother didn't raise a fool. Anything I said or did would be used against me in the future.

At the room, she held the door for me, and I nodded thanks as I set her bags next to the small dresser.

"Thanks for carrying my bags up."

I didn't give her a chance to say more. I knew a dismissal when I heard one. She wasn't getting rid of me that easily.

In less than a heartbeat, I was in her personal space with my mouth on hers. I gave her no chance to escape.

Her small gasp was all I needed for invitation to dive further. My tongue coaxed hers to dance. She tasted like chocolate and cinnamon, and smelled like need and promise.

I dropped a hand to her waist, pulling her closer even as my free hand fisted in her hair. I wanted more. I needed to feel her against me. Kissing her wasn't enough.

She shivered when I rubbed my body against hers and moaned in my mouth at the press of my cock against her stomach. My blood raced, and any thoughts outside of her were gone.

I wanted to cover her in my seed, fill her with it. Bury myself in her. Claim her as mine in ways that only a shifter would understand.

Her violent shove surprised me enough to throw me back several steps. I tried to clear my head as we stared at each other, both chests heaving. I reached out a hand, and she stepped back, raising her arms in a defensive position.

"I want you to leave." Her voice shook.

I wasn't sure I understood her words. The mountain lion roared his displeasure. Closing my eyes, I tried to focus beyond the cat and the pounding in my blood. My tongue was thick, and I sounded drunk. "You can't be serious."

"I'm not a whore."

The cat wanted to leap forward and pin her down. Actions meant more than words to the cat, but this wasn't the time or place for force.

I ignored the not-so-silent nudging and held her gaze. "I never thought you were."

"Please leave."

I shook my head. "You're insane. The bond has started. Do you know what kind of pain we'll be in if I just leave?"

"I don't know what you're talking about." Her arms wrapped around her torso in a self-hug.

"The mate bond. I know you feel it." I stepped forward, and she stepped back.

"I don't have a mate. I would need a shift for that, and I can't shift. Never could. So you're mistaken." Her tone hardened.

"You don't need a shift. That's snobbery and purity talking. You exist. That's all you need to draw a mate bond." I wanted to press her into admitting it. In another two steps, she'd be against the bed, but it wasn't just desire I smelled. She feared me, and her fear effectively killed my desire.

Her eyes shifted away. "Nicholas, please leave."

I tried to soften my tone, suddenly unsure of where I stood or why she feared me. "We can't ignore this, Audrey. That's not how the bond works."

"You're wrong!" She threw a hand toward the door. "Get out."

Actions meant more than words. I braced myself. This wasn't going to be kind to either of us.

I made it to the door before the pounding in my temples started. This was an all-around bad idea, but I couldn't force her to accept me. I wouldn't; it wasn't in my nature.

The door clicked quietly behind me. The sensation was like a rubber band being pulled too far. Eventually it would snap.

At the top of the stairs, my vision blurred and grayed as pain exploded through my body. I missed the step and tumbled down the flight. I barely felt the pain of the fall.

Someone rushed to help, but I couldn't clearly see who.

"Outside," I managed through racking spasms. I needed to get farther away before the bond tried to relink.

"You can't drive like this." Michaela's voice pierced the pain.

"Outside." I attempted to crawl toward where the door might be. I couldn't see a damn thing, not even the rays of sunshine that should be warming the floor.

She sighed, and I was hefted up from both sides—Sindi helped, too, by the smell.

In the bright light of day, the pain receded enough for me to regain some of my senses. I stumbled over to the truck and leaned against the cool metal. My head cleared a little more but the pain in my chest remained strong. It hurt to breathe—likely would until Audrey accepted or we died from denial.

"Thanks. I'm better." I turned to look at the women who followed me out. "Let her charge whatever to the room. Make sure she eats. Can you write a note for me? She's going to be looking for work."

Michaela crossed her arms. "What was that, Jordan?"

I rubbed my sore chest. "Nothing you need to worry about. It's . . . personal."

Michaela didn't look convinced, but Sindi sniffed. "You smell like sex."

"Sindi." Michaela slapped her arm.

Sindi shrugged. "What's the message?"

I sighed and hoped Audrey would accept a helping hand, as it was intended, and not consider it a handout. "Thanks. I appreciate it."

AUDREY

My morning was spent in agonized spasms. I curled up on the bed silently crying and waiting for pain worse than any injuries from my accident to pass. Even my broken ribs didn't hurt like this. My soul felt like it was being forcefully ripped from my body.

Despite Nicholas's words, despite the slap of truth, I still couldn't believe I had a mate. Everyone I encountered in the past was adamant it wouldn't happen. Snobbery and purity he had called it. I didn't want to believe him, but there was nothing else that explained the racking pain, not even the car accident.

When I could move without tears, I began the mission of finding a job. I slipped out of the inn without being seen by Michaela or Sindi. For now, I didn't want to face any personal questions. I'd have enough of them while applying for work.

The shops on the square would be a good place to start. After a frustrating two hours of nothing—even with the season starting, no one was looking for help—I returned to the inn. Michaela smiled and waved me over to the desk when she saw me.

"Here. Nicholas left you a note. And you've been granted permission to charge food to the room if you need to."

"I don't need his fucking charity." I studied the sticky note Nicholas wrote. The handwriting looked suspiciously feminine, but I doubted Michaela would lie about its origin. The directions were clear, and yet vague at the same time. I wondered what kind of person Melaina Savage was to open a club in an old mine. It certainly took a whole lot of innovation.

Michaela shrugged when I asked her what she knew about Silk, and provided alternatives—the Haven Saloon and the Dirty Knuckle —for employment. With nothing else to do with my afternoon, I went and scouted them out; options were always a good thing. I felt good about those applications and chances for employment, though the pay worried me a bit.

When night fell, I headed out once more, following Nicholas's instructions. As I walked down Main Street toward where I was assured the parking lot for the club was, I checked out the shops on the street again, and in Miller's Plaza. For such a small town, there was a surprising variety of businesses and places I could see myself using when I got back on my feet.

Despite being a strange small town, it didn't feel unsafe to walk along the road in the dark. Perhaps that was naïve of me, or maybe it was some kind of magic. I could definitely understand why people chose to live here, though. Simple night sounds filled the air, and the ski trails were lit up on the side of the mountain. The town was beautiful. Havenwood Falls felt safer than a lot of the cities I had lived in, and the air was just as crisp and beautiful as in Glacier in Montana.

Although closed for the day, the nail salon—my guilty pleasure—caught my attention, and I glanced down at the eighteen-day-old polish on my fingers. It wasn't chipped, but it was growing out. I'd have to see about that soon or take it off to remain professional looking.

The couple mile walk was over faster than I expected. Next time, I'd bring a flashlight; some of the streetlamps along the road weren't lit, and I couldn't afford to trip and add to my injuries. Until I mapped out a running path, the walk would be good to stay in shape.

I studied the gondola lift from the edges of the decently lit parking lot. My brain expected a hole in the ground, not several stories up the side of the mountain. I'd never been on a gondola before, and the idea of it gave me a bit of apprehension. I never tried roller coasters or Ferris wheels either.

I considered my options. I could wait to hear from one of Michaela's suggested places or . . . stand still. Do nothing. And those options weren't acceptable.

If I wanted to pay my debts off, I needed a good job, and in a town this size, I didn't have a lot of choices. There was no way a business would be open in the mountain if the way to get there wasn't completely safe. I released a deep breath and muttered a prayer under my breath as I approached the gondola.

A big man in a suit stood in front of the entrance, screening the people. I noticed some flashed their cell phones at him and others showed bright red business cards. The big man turned out to be one of average size when I was close to him—the benefits of being a tall woman.

He was still taller than I, though not enough that I had to tilt my head back to look in his eyes.

"Hi." I smiled at him before he could speak. "I'm here to see Melaina Savage about a job."

I couldn't see his eyes behind his sunglasses—who wore sunglasses at ten at night?—but I watched his brow furrow. "Name?"

"Audrey Smith." I chewed my lip. "I don't have an appointment or anything. I wrecked my car a couple of days ago . . ."

The wrinkle between his brows smoothed out. "Oh. You're the Challenger girl. Shame about the car. Sweet ride."

I canted my head and studied him a little closer. I didn't remember seeing him in the last few days. "How did you know that?"

"Liam was on duty. Gimme a sec." He pulled a walkie-talkie from his belt. "Ms. Savage, there's a lady down here looking for a job. The elk girl."

Static crackled on the radio before a woman responded. "Send her up."

The man put the radio back on his belt and gestured to the gondola. "Ride on up."

"Thanks."

He jerked his chin. "Hurry, before you miss this one. She doesn't like to be kept waiting."

I nodded and hurried over to the almost empty gondola. As it lurched from the ground, I reminded myself they wouldn't use it if it was a hazard. When it lifted up barely below the treetops, I found myself pressed to the glass, staring out in wonder.

The town was even prettier from above. How did anyone not ride the gondola a hundred times just to see the town from this angle? Maybe that's why Melaina built so high—to show off her town?

I wiped my damp palms over my clean black pants. There was nothing to be nervous about. My clothes were clean and professional and my hair pulled back. The ache left in the wake of Nicholas's absence was ignorable, and I knew how to do the job I wanted.

The ride was too short, and I stepped off last behind the others, not sure what to do or where to go. I realized after a moment there was only one way to go, unless I got back on the gondola. I followed the crowd down a short hall and tried not to gawk at the big beautiful doors and gorgeous front room area, or the perfectly stunning woman standing at the hostess podium.

I felt frumpy and overdressed in comparison to her tight dress and stiletto heels, but reminded myself what I wore was standard for most bartenders. Dress for the job you wanted, right? And the all-black look was flattering to a degree. Still, the woman's perfect curls and to-die-for curves didn't boost my self-esteem any.

"Excuse me." I waited for the hostess to turn her attention from the touch screen and tried to not look down on the woman. She smelled unlike anything I'd ever encountered before, so I was cautious. There were more supernaturals in the world than animal shifters, and many of them a lot more dangerous. "I'm here to see Melaina Savage."

The woman's blood red lips curved. I didn't fidget as her eyes traveled down and back up again. When she spoke, her voice came out with a sultry rasp. "I am Melaina Savage. You must be Audrey."

"Yes, ma'am." I folded my hands at my waist. "I was hoping to speak to you about a bartending job, but I can waitress, too."

She eyed me once more, her tongue sliding over her lips. "Follow me. I'm a busy woman, and I don't give handouts. You're lucky I'm short-staffed or I'd be forced to question your common sense, coming at this time of night. You want a job, I'm willing to give you a chance, but you have to earn it." Melaina turned from the podium and headed into the main space. "Our main area has several bars, lounge spaces, some tables. You see the dance floor. This main area is open to the public—as long as they pay the hefty cover charge. Invitations for private events are coveted by the rich. We're in season right now, so hours of operation are nine to three. Every day. You'll get two days off a week, depending on business needs. At the moment, those days will be Tuesday and Sunday. Those are subject to change."

Melaina smiled and nodded at patrons as we walked through the main space and up a short four steps, past two bouncers and into another smaller bar area that looked out over the main space—everyone's eyes following her. I forced myself to keep pace with Melaina instead of staring. The transformation was incredible. No one would ever guess the club wasn't the intended purpose of the cavern. Silk could rival any club on the Las Vegas Strip.

"This is VIP." Melaina held open the bar swing. "Consider this a working resume. Impress me and we'll get your paperwork done at the end of the shift. Disappoint and I'll pay you in cash, and tonight never happened."

I nodded and stepped through to the bar. Melaina pointed to the bouncers. "If you get into shit, just whistle. The guys will come to your rescue."

"Yes, ma'am."

"Good. I'll be back at the end of the night. Help should show up around mid-shift to give you a break." Melaina sauntered away without any further directive.

I glanced around, noting that while VIP wasn't busy, it wasn't dead either. I took notice of drinks on tables and the two men at the bar as I made myself at home behind it. This was my comfort zone, and I had no problem with Melaina's test.

CHAPTER 6

NICHOLAS

The bright bouquet of flowers on the passenger seat mocked me. Reagan, owner at Fairy Tale Florists, insisted the irises and carnations were a perfect mix for a first date. Shifters didn't need the flounce and preamble of courtship, a mate was a mate, and yet . . . I found myself about to propose just that. My mate—I refused to call her anything else—had better appreciate the effort I put in. I didn't want to go through another restless night.

She had no shift, though I wondered why, since the cat was on the surface of her scent.

The thought didn't bother me. As I picked up the flowers and slammed out of the truck, I wondered why it bothered her. Then again, the outside world didn't have the safety of Havenwood Falls' rules. Rules could be broken, of course, but the consequences were dire. I lost a friend to broken rules, and Dad's best friend lost three children.

I pulled myself out of past memories as I entered the inn. Sindi gave me a once-over and smirked at the flowers. "You're seriously going this route at eight o'clock in the morning?"

I ignored her and headed up the stairs. Yes, this wasn't the greatest of ideas. However, I didn't have to explain my lack of reasoning to anyone but Audrey. And if I couldn't sleep, why should she be able to?

After a deep breath, I knocked on Audrey's door. When no noise came from the other side, I knocked a little harder. As I knocked for the third time, rattling the door in its frame, my mind went over our possible future once she accepted facts.

Would she like the cabin? I didn't live fancy, but it was a nice cabin. My ancestor built it when he arrived in the valley some hundred years ago. Would it be big enough?

How many kids did she want? What if she didn't want kids? All shifters wanted kids; it was part of our nature . . . but she wasn't raised like other shifters. I pushed the worrisome thought away to address later. I had to win the girl first—a ridiculous thought for a mountain lion shifter, but it was what it was.

Maybe she slept as heavily as I did? Our poor cubs would have a hell of a time getting to school if that was the case. Mr. Brauner didn't stand for tardiness, and was even more of a stickler about it since becoming principal of the elementary school.

The door popped open when I lifted my hand to pound once again, and I was grateful she gave me a minute to find my voice. My cat purred in delight, and all my muscles tightened. This morning's cold shower no longer held its sway over my dick, and I went rock hard in seconds. I closed my eyes, but the damage was already done.

Audrey's robe slid off one shoulder, revealing blushing, pale skin and a thin tank underneath. She didn't have any pants covering her legs, and her hair looked tousled from sleep. Her voice was rough, almost hoarse, when she spoke. "What do you want?"

I held out the flowers and took a breath, instantly wishing I hadn't. She smelled like sex and the toiletries I gave her. The cat immediately screamed his displeasure. She wasn't allowed to smell that way unless we were involved.

Her hand reached out for the bouquet, and the smell of sex strengthened. I couldn't stop myself from grabbing her wrist with my other hand and lifting her fingers to my nose. I kept my eyes on her face as my tongue darted out and licked her digits. She tasted fresh and sweet. A single sample wasn't anywhere close to enough to satisfy me.

She froze as I cleaned her essence off her hand. Her eyes half closed, her chest heaved, and her nipples poked through the thin robe. I could smell her fresh desire. She wasn't immune to me. That gave me hope.

"Did you think of me when you fingered yourself? Did you moan my name as you came?" I licked her again, wishing I could drop to my knees and drown in her juices. I nearly did just that, but Audrey surprised me.

She jerked away, and the door slammed in my face. I fought my instinct to break down the door and chase her down. I rested my head against the smooth wood and sighed. "Audrey. Audrey, this isn't easy."

A finger tapped my shoulder, and I turned my head to see a teenage girl looking at me—by the smell of her, a wolf—and I almost snarled. I was so focused on Audrey I hadn't noticed her creeping up on me.

She looked like she belonged on a farm somewhere with her cowboy boots and hat. She rolled her eyes and held out her phone so I could see what she wrote.

Your game sucks. Flowers aren't going to fix this.

She pulled her phone back and began typing away before turning it once more.

Try being a little more conscious of her feelings instead of yours. It's obvious what you want.

I rolled my eyes. "What does a teenage girl know?"

"So much for subtle." She lifted a brow and crossed her arms. "I'm not the one on the wrong side of the door with raging pheromones making the air difficult for others to breathe. Try being sensitive male instead of primitive male. It might work better."

"Iris." A college-aged male version of the teen, right down to the boots, stood at the top of the stairs. "I thought you wanted to see if the slopes were open yet."

"Coming, Theo." She shook her head at me. "You need work."

I watched her go down the stairs and the man, another unfamiliar wolf shifter, tipped his hat at me. "Sorry about her. She's a romantic at heart. Good luck with your girl." He disappeared down the stairs.

I was almost embarrassed by the altercation. I'd never expected getting my mate to like me would be so hard. As a rule, mates understood and accepted they belonged together, but Audrey was different.

"Audrey." I rested my hand on the door, and my words died on my tongue. That smart-ass kid's snark still echoed in the air. "Audrey, I'm sorry. You're beautiful, and . . . I lost my head. I can't promise control. I wish I could."

"What do you want?" She sounded like she leaned against the door from the other side.

"I thought we could go out. Like on a date. Get to know each other." My cat and dick both protested any form of delay, but Audrey needed to be handled with kid gloves. The teen, Iris, was right about that. If Audrey ran from the town, I would have no future.

"Shifters don't date." Curiosity tinged her voice.

I frowned. "How do you know?"

"I stayed in a commune for a while around Lake Tahoe. They tried to help me figure out why I couldn't shift. It was . . . educating, among other things."

The way she hesitated, I thought there might be more story behind the commune experience. "Well, if you change your mind and would like to skip the human ritual—" My cat agreed with that line of thinking.

The door popped open a second, and Audrey snatched the flowers out of my hand. "Come back in six hours." The door slammed again.

I rested a hand on the door and shook my head. I wanted to push the issue. I didn't want to wait, but . . . Audrey wanted me to come back later. Her agreement was progress, wasn't it?

Bemused, I conceded and made for the stairs. At least I had secured the date. If I could convince her our lives depended on our bond, the pain in my chest might be resolved by the time the moon rose.

"If you had asked," Sindi began when she spotted me on the stairs, "I'd have told you she didn't come in until around four. She went out to Silk last night."

That explained her request for six hours. Audrey was going back to bed. I wished my mind hadn't conjured the image of her in bed, touching herself, while thinking of me. I had no doubt she thought of me. I certainly did a lot of thinking about her. If we didn't come to terms soon, I might lose my damn mind before the end of the week.

"Good luck." Sindi's laughter followed me out.

Audrey was being a stubborn ass. I was going to need all the luck I could get.

~

AUDREY

I SIPPED my black coffee as Nicholas stirred sugar and cream in his. He sat across from me at a little table in front of the windows at Coffee Haven. After yesterday's vicious slap of agony when Nicholas left, I intended to keep my distance, yet here I was. A headache that bordered on migraine remained, and I had a feeling it would be with me until I did something about the man.

Nicholas wasn't hard to look at. I blamed his prettiness for my inability to fall right back to sleep after he left. Hours later, I could still feel his tongue on my hand, and imagine all the better ways it could be put to use. My panties soaked through at the very idea of his tongue on my clit, and I averted my gaze when his eyes landed on me. Damn the man's sense of smell. The damn flowers were at fault for my decision to go on a date. I should have stayed in bed with all my dirty thoughts and the privacy to release the tension they created.

With all the traveling I did, getting to know someone was impractical, and I missed out on the little nuances of certain rituals. Shifters didn't date, but they did show affection. The flowers—now in a place of honor on the little desk in my room—softened me more than I cared to admit. Before I could think of how to start the conversation we needed to have, an older woman stopped next to our table.

"Hello, Nicholas dear." The older lady set down a plate with two muffins on it.

"Hello, Ms. Half-Moon. What can I do for you?" Nicholas smiled and leaned back in his chair.

The old woman's eyes landed on me a moment before focusing on Nicholas. "Oh, nothing, sweetheart. I brought you some muffins. I wanted to thank you for all the hard work you put in for this community. It seems every time something happens, there you are, swooping in for the rescue. You and the sheriff, of course."

The woman placed her hand on Nicholas's shoulder. For some reason, that single action rubbed me wrong, and I was ready to tear into the old lady for touching him. I took a deep breath. Nicholas was his own person. Despite the pull to him, I had no claim.

"I am a licensed paramedic. It's kind of in the job description, Ms. Half-Moon." Nicholas sipped his coffee. When he glanced in my direction over the rim, he winked.

"Well, we're lucky to have you." Ms. Half-Moon squeezed Nicholas's shoulder, and I ground my teeth. She smiled at me. "Who is this lovely young lady?"

"Audrey." I forced a smile, trying hard not to bare my teeth at the woman. "I've only recently come to town."

"Well, welcome to Havenwood Falls, honey. Have you had a chance to wander around and take in our wonderfully eccentric town? You should show her around, Nicholas." She let go of Nicholas and turned to fully face me.

"Just between us—" Nicholas touched Ms. Half-Moon's arm to get her attention and lowered his voice— "someone mentioned an end-of-the-year fundraiser for the public services and I overheard it could be a bachelor auction. All the single public servants are supposed to be participating. I heard the sheriff complain, but promised to do his duty, if it does occur."

"Oh, my, well." Ms. Half-Moon fanned her reddening face. "That would be . . . swell." She glanced at the watch on her wrist. "Oh, look at that. I'm sorry to cut this short, dearies, but I've got a girls' date set up with Irene for this afternoon. I'm going to be late."

"Of course, Ms. Half-Moon. You have a good time. You tell Irene I said hello." His grin widened when she fluttered a wave at him and hurried out of the coffee shop.

I narrowed my eyes at him. "You said that on purpose."

Nicholas rolled his eyes. "She was only over here for you. I've bought you some time before she comes back to snoop some more. There's very little that goes on in Havenwood Falls that she doesn't know about."

"So, how did she not know about the auction?"

Nicholas reached for a muffin and sniffed it. "Banana nut. The auction isn't official yet. It's one of many ideas we're throwing around for fundraising this year. It may not even happen. Though, now that Biddie knows, it has a better chance."

I took the other muffin on the plate when he pushed it my way. "Aren't you worried?"

He lifted a brow. "No. If we don't mate, I'll be dead before then. So will you. And if we do mate, I won't be single."

I choked on the muffin and grabbed my coffee to wash it down. "You don't know that."

Nicholas tapped a finger against his temple. "The pain hasn't gone away. How long do you think we have until it drives one of us, or both of us, mad? What do you think happens to an out of control shifter?"

I opened my mouth to respond, but closed it.

The commune shifters called them ferals. Ferals were collared and caged. Lawbreakers were put in the cage with them. No one came out of a cage alive. Not even the feral. I didn't know what would happen in Havenwood Falls, but since I'd already met the sheriff, I could guess. He didn't take a threat to Havenwood Falls lightly.

"Come on. This is only one shop on the square. Havenwood Falls is actually a really nice little town." Nicholas stood and stretched.

"I saw a nail salon in the plaza. I wanted to get my nails painted before going back to work tonight." I followed him out, holding what remained of my coffee.

I debated stepping away when he placed a hand on the small of my back, but it felt like a petty move. Besides, a simple touch wouldn't hurt anything, would it? I pretended the ever present migraine didn't fade when he touched me.

"We can go that way." When Nicholas paused to put his sunglasses on, the hairs on the back of my neck stood up.

I scanned the area. Despite not having a shift, my senses were keen and had never let me down before. A few people walked on the sidewalk, but nothing seemed out of sorts. Across the street in the square, a couple of blond teens wrestled on the snow and a few others threw a football back and forth. The scene looked completely normal.

"Something wrong?" Nicholas gave a cursory glance over the area.

"It's silly. Felt like I was being watched." I tried pushing the feeling away, but I still couldn't get past the sensation. I stepped away from his hand, suddenly uncomfortable with the idea of him touching me in public. The immediate return of the mild headache made me almost regret the action.

"Probably are." Nicholas turned in the direction of the plaza and set off at a stroll without comment on my action. "You're a new face in town, and I haven't been seen with a woman since a close friend of mine died. I wouldn't take it seriously."

"I'm sorry about your friend." I couldn't think of anything else to say. Instead I reached out for his hand and squeezed his fingers. When I pulled my hand back, Nicholas held on.

"It's in the past." Nicholas's tone hardened. "It won't happen again."

We walked hand in hand, in silence for a moment. It almost felt normal, and my heart cracked. I couldn't have normal—*I* wasn't normal—but he deserved it.

"Why haven't you called me instead of walking to work?" Nicholas hit the crosswalk button on the street light.

"The walk is fine." I shrugged and wished the light would turn faster.

"You're injured."

"You're stubborn. Pick your battles, Nicholas. You're not going to win this one."

"I could walk with you if you insist on walking. You could catch a

47

ride with one of the other employees." He canted his body to look down at me.

"We're walking now, and I'm fine." I resisted the urge to growl at him. The man was a nuisance at times.

"It's not as far as Silk."

I nearly ran forward when the light finally cleared us to walk. The sensation of being watched faded when we crossed the block and passed the apartment buildings. Despite being out on the public sidewalk, our stroll felt more intimate than it should have been.

"Thank you for Melaina's information." I changed the subject, hoping he would let the topic of my transportation go.

"Sure. I do little odds and ends stuff for her brother, Savage, and Liam, who's like a brother to her, works on a voluntary basis with me. She's always looking for good help, according to the guys." Nicholas waved when someone shouted his name but kept walking.

"You sure are popular." I sniffed and wished I hadn't.

With him this close, I got a nose full of his scent. He smelled delicious, like sin and smoke. The aroma went to my head like a drug. All the things we could do together raced through my mind and made the body aches I thought I had under control return full force.

Nicholas leaned over and whispered in my ear. "I don't know what you're thinking about, but unless you're trying to get me to fuck you in a back alley, you need to stop."

I blinked and took a calming breath through my suddenly dry mouth. I hadn't realized we had stopped walking or that my heart raced a mile a minute. I felt my cheeks heat under Nicholas's scrutiny, but didn't look at him as I began moving again. "Sorry."

"What were you thinking about?" He didn't miss a beat and grabbed my hand before I got too far from him.

"Doesn't matter. You said you wanted me to stop thinking about it." We turned into the plaza as I wiped my mind blank of all salacious thoughts.

"I changed my mind." He didn't let go when I tugged on my hand.

"Well, too late." I reached for the door to the salon, but Nicholas beat me to it.

"Ladies first." He let my hand go and followed to the reception desk.

The shop was relatively empty. I noted the woman getting a pedicure, and two others getting nails done. In Reno, the nail salons were never empty; it was a welcome change.

"Welcome. What service today?" The technician seemed a little annoyed, if the way she flipped her dark hair to reveal the neon red underneath was any indication. To my relief, her accent wasn't so heavy she couldn't be understood.

I held out my hand to show the grown out nails. "Just a manicure."

"One manicure. You get anything?" The technician looked over at Nicholas.

"Not today." Nicholas dug out some cash and handed the bills to the technician. "But I'm more than happy to pay for my lady."

I sputtered as the technician accepted the cash. "You can't just . . . I'm not your lady."

"Pick color, and come to table four." The technician waved a hand at the double-sided wall of nail polish bottles between the waiting area and the manicure tables before moving away.

"You are, and I can. Get over it." Nicholas walked over to the nail polishes.

"I don't think you understand." I grabbed his arm when Nicholas ignored me to pick up colors and compare them.

My breath caught when he turned his head and met my gaze. I felt butterflies in my stomach and couldn't move when he leaned over close enough to kiss me, if he wanted to.

"This isn't going away, kitten. No matter how much you want it to. Get used to it. You need to wrap your head around it? Fine, but there's a ticking clock on how long you can pretend you don't feel the draw." His breath tickled my face, and I couldn't stop myself from leaning in a little.

He stepped back and handed me a bottle of polish. "I like this one."

I shook off the haze of need he created, and accepted the bottle.

Instead of arguing with him, I studied the color. I wanted to argue, to tell him he was wrong, but . . . But the ache in my soul, the nagging headache, and my uncontrollable reaction when in proximity to him said otherwise.

The bronze was somewhere between metallic and glitter. A perfect, low key, autumn color. I hated that he knew what I wanted without me saying anything. Frustration, fear, and sorrow all mixed together, and tears welled in my eyes.

"I just don't understand." I sat down at the table where the technician waited.

"I am Dao. Hands in water. Real nails or acrylic?" Dao accepted the bottle of color and pulled out tools while my hands soaked.

"You said you stayed in a commune." Nicholas lowered his voice and tipped his chin at the women two tables over as he sat in the vacant chair next to me. "Non-supes."

"These are real." I focused on Dao instead of looking at Nicholas. I matched his lowered tone. "Yes, but there were a handful of . . . mixed couples—primarily ignored—but for the most part, like with like. And no one talked to me about mating. We talked about why I couldn't shift and how to fix that."

"We have the same soul animal, I'm sure of that." Nicholas shrugged. "I don't care whether you do or not, but for some reason you're fixated on the fact you can't shift."

"It's taboo. You need a strong mate that can provide strong children." I scowled at him.

"Out here anything goes, and if we met out there, it would be the same. Fate has spoken. You're swimming against the current, Audrey."

"I don't understand how you can just accept. How is it fair that we don't have a choice?" I shook my head. How could he be so accepting? We were strangers.

"We have a legend in China." Dao spoke softly and clearly, startling me. She reached up into her bob and pulled out a long red hair. "It is said the god Yue Lao ties the red string of fate to those that are destined." Dao made tiny slip knots in each end of the strand. She looped one end over the pinky finger of my right hand and the other end over Nicholas's left pinky when he set his hand on the table at her gesture. "The string can stretch and twist, but it will never break. You complain about choice, but the gods have chosen you for each other. No one knows you better then they. Some of us will never have what you do here. Not because it doesn't exist, but because we never get the chance to meet. The Americans call it something else—soul mates."

"Nothing is forever." I jerked my hand and was surprised when the thin hair held and didn't break.

Dao smiled. "It can stretch and twist, but you cannot break the gods' will. You are destined, and for your species, that is forever."

"We don't know each other," I growled and pulled on my hand again. Still the hair stubbornly remained whole. Did she have steel hair?

"You have forever to learn what the gods already know." Dao took my hand and unlooped the hair from my finger and Nicholas's.

Before I could sort my thoughts, a siren went off, making me jolt. Nicholas cursed and pulled out a cell phone. The noise stopped when he swiped the screen. He scanned the screen and sighed.

"I have to go. Duty calls. Be good for Dao." He leaned over and placed an innocent kiss on the top of my head as he stood.

I watched him walk away, and a vise clamped around my heart. He paused at the door before stepping out. The stabbing pain was instant. My eyes closed, and I focused on breathing through the invisible agony.

"The gods do not like to be ignored." Dao's voice penetrated through the fog.

"I suppose not." I kept my eyes closed as Dao worked. The pain wasn't as bad as last time. Maybe the fact that he hadn't really touched me kept the pain to a minimum.

I wished I had someone I could talk to about it. Even if I was in the commune, no one there would talk about it. They made it seem that without the shift, the mate bond would never happen. Never in my life did I feel more alone.

CHAPTER 7

NICHOLAS

The call hadn't been a major one, but I left Audrey to stew in her thoughts for a while instead of returning to her side like I wanted. She had an inferiority complex she needed to get past. For both our sakes.

As I pulled into Silk's parking lot, I saw Audrey step off the gondola platform and walk along the edges of the pavement. My timing couldn't have been better, if she was on a break. I hurried to park and intercept her on her walk.

Audrey's unique smell drew me like a moth to a flame. I could find her blindfolded if I was so inclined. She could likely do the same for me if she wanted to. When her posture stiffened, I smiled. She *could* sniff me out if she wanted to.

"How's your night going?" I matched my stride to hers and was secretly delighted I didn't have to check my steps any.

Audrey sighed and rubbed her temples. She subtly shifted away and her musk filled the air. Her physical response to my proximity gave me hope for our future. In my experience, there was only so long lust could be ignored.

"It isn't going to go away that way." I stepped in front of her and held out my hand.

Audrey stared at my hand and shook her head. "It's not a good idea."

"It's the only idea, Audrey. We're running out of time. My cat's growing more and more impatient. I don't think I'll be in control by the end of the week." My voice dropped, mindful that not everyone in the area was supernatural.

I hated admitting I wasn't in full control, but mating was an act between two. Even if I broke the promise to myself and forced her hand, she had to be willing for the deal to seal.

Her eyes darted to my face, searching. I waited while she studied me. After a long moment of hesitation, she dropped her hand into my waiting one.

My eyes drifted closed, and some of the tension faded from my muscles. "I need you to make a decision. I need to know if I should be saying goodbye to my family and turning myself in to Ric. I don't want to put the town in danger because I'm out of control."

Her voice shook a little. "What if I left?"

My eyes snapped open. "Are you out of your fucking mind? The cat is difficult to control now. If you leave . . . there's no pretense of control."

Audrey flinched. "I just thought—"

I pinned her against the closest car, pressing my body against hers. My cock stood at attention, hard and aching against her pelvis. A startled gasp escaped her, allowing me to dip in and plunder her parted lips with my tongue. One of us moaned, and Audrey's free hand fisted the fabric of my shirt.

The parking lot was lit, but not well enough that I worried much about the bouncer at the gondola seeing us, nor did I worry about some random club-goer. Since the club still had several business hours remaining, I doubted anyone would come along and catch us in a publicly indecent position.

I pressed my entire body against hers, never releasing her mouth, needing more contact. I could feel the desperation in myself, and wanted her to feel just as out of control. I needed her to feel as needy as I did.

I nipped her bottom lip with my teeth as I ran kisses down the side of her neck. "I've changed my mind. I'm not going to let you kill us. You come to me within twenty-four hours. If not, I'm coming to you. No more running away, Audrey. And don't even fucking think about leaving."

"I don't— I can't—" The haze of lust blurred her eyes, and I kissed her again, because I could.

My hand drifted down along the tight black shirt she wore and teased the edges of the fabric where it rode up away from her pants. She shuddered when my fingers touched her bare flesh and automatically shifted, opening her stance a little more when my fingers teased under the waistband of her pants.

"Nicholas."

I wasn't sure if my name was a prayer or a curse when my hand dipped deeper into her pants and cupped her dripping pussy. A low growl rumbled in my chest as I ran a finger through slick folds. When I rubbed her clit in a hard circle, Audrey gasped, her head fell back, and her hands grabbed at my waist. I pressed the little button a little harder, and she moaned, thrusting her hips against my hand.

"You're not exactly fighting me off, kitten." My tongue traced the curve of her ear. "As much as I would love to drag you home and claim you right now, I think Melaina would skin me and use me for a rug if I tried. She's not a woman to cross."

As much as it hurt me to, I pulled away, stepping back far enough to release myself from her hold. Audrey's hand lifted to reach out, before she caught herself and pulled back. I watched her struggle to contain her desire.

When she finally found her voice, her tone was soft and unsteady. "You deserve better."

I shook my head. "I deserve you."

"You don't know me." She didn't push me away when I rested my forehead against hers.

"I trust my instincts. You should trust yours more. If you want, just think of it as an arranged marriage. I'll even get you a human ring if you want. Those kind of arrangements are still in practice today." My kiss was gentle, teasing . . . promising but no less potent. I consumed her, knowing she would taste me long after I left her for the night.

When I pulled away, I felt drugged and muddled. "Twenty-four hours, kitten. I will come find you. We can't keep doing this, and I have no intentions of dying this young."

I walked back to my truck, aching with need and demand. The cat pressed against my will, fighting for control. We'd go for a run, and hopefully that would soothe the beast enough for tonight. I couldn't look back at her as I left her behind.

~

AUDREY

I waved at my last customer as Emiko escorted him away from my bar. Other than the constant ache in my muscles, which was completely Nicholas's fault, I had a good night. My heavy pocket promised a good tip amount, and every little bit would be needed if Joshua found the decent vehicle he promised.

The to-do list ran through my head as I cleaned up and closed down the VIP bar. Maybe I could avoid Nicholas, somehow, and let all this fade and blow over. The thought of him made my entire body pulse and ache. The pounding in my head increased—a little more insistent. I closed my eyes and took a deep breath, focusing on the rest of my things to do instead of the man.

After I took the dirties to the kitchen, picked up some cleans, and came back to the bar, I found Melaina waiting on a stool. My boss made everyone work hard, but she was fair. Despite not knowing much about her, I liked the always gorgeous woman.

"Hey, boss. You need me?" I grinned as I put the tray of clean glasses on the bar and refilled the station. Despite my smile, being alone with her made me edgy, and I couldn't quite put my finger on why.

"The bouncers have noticed your habit of walking to and from work." Melaina crossed her arms, her gaze traveling over me as though drinking me in. Even without meaning to, the woman exuded sex, which didn't help the ache in my already needy body. "How long do you plan on being in Havenwood Falls?"

My brows drew together as I reset the alcohol bottles. "I'll be here a while. The insurance is being difficult. I have to pay for a new car and . . ." I didn't say his name, but I needed to figure out what to do about the driving need to be with Nicholas. Pretty soon, I'd be humping his leg instead of wetting my panties every time he was close.

"And you have a mate you're refusing to accept. You want to fuck him, but for some reason, you deny him and yourself." Melaina's nostrils flared, as though she could smell the desire on me, and she held up a hand before I could even begin to protest. "Nicholas Jordan is an asset to this community. Denying a mate ends in death for both parties. You do know that, right?"

I shrugged and winced at the throbbing reminder that my shoulder was still healing. A real shifter would have healed by now. It was another reminder I wasn't good enough for Nicholas. "I don't want to cause any trouble, Melaina. Nicholas is mistaken. Fate wouldn't bind him to an orphan mate with no shift. As the asset to the community you say he is, we both know he deserves better than me."

Melaina tilted her head. "Who are you to decide if fate is wrong or right? But I digress. You're walking, alone, which isn't smart by the way, back and forth to Whisper Falls Inn."

I looked away from my boss and went back to my work. Since she knew about the car accident, I didn't see a point in reminding her about the lack of transportation. "It's a nice walk. I don't know where the running paths are, so the walk is a good way to stay in shape."

Melaina's perfectly polished nails tapped on the wooden bar top, and her face was unreadable. Something about the seriousness of her expression set me on edge. The boss, while serious, wasn't usually difficult for me to read.

My stomach pitched, and I forced my hands to go still before Melaina could see them shaking. "Am I being fired?"

"I could. If I did, I'd ask Savage to go with you to the inn, pack your bags, and take you out to Durango." Melaina looked down at the phone in her hand and sent a couple of text messages while I digested the statement.

Icy fingers ran down my spine. "You're going to force me to leave?"

"I could . . . but that would be disastrous. Not just for Silk." She smiled in a way that made me shift from foot to foot. The woman was up to something, but what, she kept to herself. "You're done for the night, right?" Melaina glanced around the bar. "Good job. Come." The way she said it, with her always sultry voice and the seductive twist of her body, the word sounded like an order to orgasm, and I could easily imagine many people—regardless of gender—doing so on her simple command. She just had that way about her. Then she added more curtly, "With me."

With dread pitting in my stomach, I grabbed my purse from under the bar and followed. What would I do if Melaina did have me taken out of town? What *could* I do? Would the insurance still pay out? I hadn't asked if I had to stay in place; I only assumed I did. And it wasn't like I had anywhere to go anyway.

What about Nicholas? Would he follow and leave Havenwood Falls without his service? His control was already slipping. Would he survive long enough to find me again?

Melaina sighed and glanced over her shoulder. "You're not being fired, Audrey. Your anxiety is giving me a headache."

"If I'm not being fired, where are we going?" I climbed onto the gondola with Melaina and stood next to the window so I could see the town as we descended. The lights were as beautiful as they were the first time.

Melaina's brows rose. "You know, so many don't enjoy the view. Such a pity. I find it a turn-on."

"Most are drunk or easily sickened by the motion."

"Touché." Melaina typed away on her phone as we descended to the parking lot.

At the bottom, I jumped out as soon as the doors opened. The bouncer nodded when I passed him and waited at the bottom of the platform stairs for Melaina. Tension still coursed through my muscles; I didn't like surprises.

I turned toward the trees on the east side of the parking lot. Nicholas was there, just beyond the tree line. I didn't see him, but could feel his presence.

"He waits for you, does he?" Melaina tipped her chin toward the trees I stared at.

I began to deny it, but the subtle movement in the trees answered Melaina for me.

"I don't suppose you noticed your entire body automatically turned in his direction when you stepped off the gondola? This way." Melaina pulled out a set of keys, and the headlights of a chrome Navigator flashed. "Probably good I drove the truck. There was a mention of snow in the forecast, but the weather has been contrary."

I said nothing about the monstrous vehicle as I climbed up into it. There was nothing about the SUV I identified as a truck. I fidgeted as Melaina drove toward the inn. "Can I ask what's going on?"

"You're staying at the inn. Not an inexpensive choice of housing. You need to save money for a car."

I gazed out the window without answering. Melaina didn't need to know about the check-in debacle. "I didn't see any cheaper rentals in the paper. And with the ski season upon us, I'm likely not going to find anything else affordable."

"False. My girls are important to me. Happy girls make happy employees. Happy employees make for really good business. I'm a fair business owner and a shrewd enough woman to know what drives my market. There's a room for rent in one of the houses I own in town. It's closer to work in a way; you can cut through the forest without Jordan having to stalk you from its shadows. If you choose. You could also ignore him altogether by following the streets." Melaina pulled into the parking lot for Whisper Falls Inn. "Pack up, check out. Don't take all morning. I have other things to do."

I turned to my boss instead of climbing out of the car. "Melaina, I really appreciate the offer—"

Melaina's smile was predatory. "It's not up for discussion. If you want to stay in town, go get your bags. My brother isn't that difficult for me to get a hold of. Your decision, of course."

With the second ultimatum of the night hanging over my head, I couldn't do anything else but comply. I sighed as I got out and went into the inn. I didn't have much to pack up—the trunk was still mostly packed, and I always put away the electronics at the end of my day, so nothing was left out. Checking out took more time than carting my things down the stairs. I tucked the receipt in my purse to give to Nicholas when I saw him next.

Melaina said nothing about the light amount of luggage I piled into the backseat of the Navigator. She put the SUV in drive before I had my seat belt back on. She began talking when we were back on Main Street. "Rent is four hundred a month for your room. You don't share the room, and all the furnishings are provided. There's a jack-and-jill bathroom you'll share with Liberty, who's in the room next to yours. Rent includes all utilities and a cleaning service that cleans the main areas of the house twice a week. Your room is your responsibility. I expect you to respect my property in the same manner you respect the bar property."

My head whirled as Melaina navigated through the streets of Havenwood Falls.

"Of course." I couldn't think of anything else to say.

"You can choose to pay me from your tips in cash, or I can take it from your check. Check would be an after-tax deduction. The girls rotate cooking for each other. I expect you to be sociable and pull your weight. You'll do your own laundry—there's a washer and dryer off the kitchen. There is no fighting in my house. If I hear of it, you're out. If you have a situation that is tense—you are all girls, after all, so it's bound to happen—I expect you to address it like responsible adults." Melaina pulled into a driveway and threw the SUV in park.

"Makes sense. I guess just take it out of my check." I stared up at the house. The porch light illuminated enough of the house to notice it looked like a normal two-story home with a bright fire-engine-red door. I looked around, and the house looked typical of an off-downtown area. "Where are we? I'm not really familiar with town."

"We're on McFeeny. The schools are at the end of the street to the west. Work is also to the west, and the town square is at the end of the street to the east. You'll get used to it. I don't restrict guests—you are grown adults—but I expect you to be respectful of each other's space and business. I honestly don't expect you to live out here more than a few days, but we'll see. Any other questions?" Melaina turned in her seat to look at me.

"No. Not really." I gazed up at the house instead of at Melaina. She wouldn't care if I voiced distress over living with other people, so why bother? In the past, I never made any friends or stuck around long enough to be memorable. And the nightmares—what would happen the first time I woke up screaming?

"One of the private room managers has the master bedroom on the first floor. He's gayer than George Takei, so you don't have to worry about that. Even as a manager at work, he has no authority to overstep in my house. You let me know if he does, but the girls generally love him." Melaina pulled out her phone and rapid-fired a text.

"Okay." There was nothing else to say. I jumped out and grabbed my stuff from the back. Sometimes the sad stack of belongings made me angry I didn't have more. In the present moment, however, I was grateful I didn't have to ask for help.

When I was two steps from the front door, it swung open, and a bronze-skinned woman stood in its frame. Her pants were so tight, her ovaries should hold a protest. She cracked a piece of gum before smiling. "Welcome. I'm Liberty."

The Navigator tooted, and the woman waved around me. For the half second of motion, I caught a glimpse of a long curly ponytail. "Let's get you in and settled. Melaina sent a text. Come on in."

Liberty stepped back, holding the door. Her smile never wavered. I straightened my shoulders and stepped inside. I could learn to be a friend. How hard could it be to deal with people in the house day in and day out? I already missed the noisy room at the inn.

CHAPTER 8

AUDREY

*L*iberty took the suitcase before leading the way through the house. She waved at a couple of girls in the kitchen before they climbed the stairs. "They work in the private areas of Silk. You'll probably only ever see them at home."

"Okay." After the work night, and Nicholas's havoc, I was too tired to hold a conversation. Thankfully, Liberty kept moving, and I only had a moment to nod an acknowledgment.

"Here's your room." Liberty opened a door and waited for me to enter.

I glanced around before setting the trunk next to the dresser. The room was an almost identical copy to the inn—bed, dresser, nightstand. The colors were different, and the room itself might have been a little smaller, but it was homey.

"Bathroom's through here." Liberty opened a door next to the closet doors. "I've already cleaned up for the morning. You can use it."

"Thanks." I knelt next to the trunk and popped it open.

Liberty sat cross-legged on the bed and watched. "Girl, your pheromones are crazy high."

My hand fisted on the nightshirt I reached for. I gave Liberty a glance. "What?"

"Pheromones. No wonder Melaina has you up front. You'd drive a supe crazy inside five minutes. How can you stand being that horny? Why haven't you taken your mate? I mean, I assume that's why your pheromones are off the chart. That's the only reason a shifter's pheromones go crazy. That and the mating season. Oh my goddess, are you in heat?"

Fire burned in my cheeks, and I could only stare at her.

Liberty crossed her arms. "We're all some kind of supernatural in the house. Secrets are a bit harder to keep here."

"I can't be in heat. I don't have a shift. And I obviously don't have a mate, for that same reason."

Liberty tipped her head. "From my understanding, you don't have to be a shifter to be a shifter's mate. The right human can be a mate."

I shifted my gaze away. "Nicholas said nearly the same thing."

"Nicholas? As in Jordan, the sexy paramedic?"

"You know him?" I turned and faced Liberty.

"Of him. The MC guys know him, but he's not actually part of the MC. Around the time I arrived in town, he left for Denver to get his state certification. I don't know the rules inside and out, but I'm pretty sure he had to get special permission to leave and come back. He'll probably get the same permission when it comes time for renewal."

"Oh. MC? What's that?" I hated asking, but better to be in the know than in the dark.

"Motorcycle club. I dated one of the guys on-again, off-again for a bit. For beings of questionable morals, they still retain some virtues. Sort of." Liberty rubbed her arms and stood up. "Look at me. Jabbering away and you still haven't showered or changed yet. I'll leave you to it. See you in a few hours."

Liberty walked out through the bathroom, leaving me to wonder what just happened. I was by no means an expert in relationships, but I would swear on my savings Liberty had a relationship problem. I had my own relationship problems, and didn't need to borrow any more.

I stared at the door Liberty disappeared through, and then the bed. I was bone-tired and wondered if some silent goddess I didn't know about would be offended if I just climbed in and dropped to sleep. Or at least tried to drop to sleep. I almost prayed for nightmares, instead of the perpetual state of lust.

Sighing with a little regret, I climbed to my feet with my toiletries and entered the bathroom. I didn't marvel at the double sink, or deep porcelain tub. I wanted to wash and pass out.

Seconds into the shower, the bathroom door creaked. "How's the water?"

I rolled my eyes. "Wet?"

"Good. Hopefully hot, too. With five of us in the house, the hot water doesn't usually survive after the back-to-back showers." Through the frosted shower curtain, I watched Liberty sit down in her doorway.

"What are you doing?" I tried not to be embarrassed by the lack of privacy.

"Talking to you. I did some thinking."

"In the whole two minutes we've been apart?" I returned my attention to my shower, since Liberty was set on staying and talking. I was careful with the soap. As I learned yesterday morning, orgasm did not provide relief—it only made the desire worse.

"I'm like the mother hen here. All the girls will say it. I'm even called Mom on occasion. It doesn't bother me in the least, and honestly I think everyone's happy with me as the house mom figure. You seem like a nice person, and down to earth, but I gotta say, I'm confused why Melaina would let you stay here with us." Liberty propped her arms up on her knees.

I froze in the shower. "What do you mean?"

"You're deliberately ignoring a mate. The longer you're here, the more dangerous the situation gets. I mean, how long do you think it's going to take before primal instincts take over? You're shifters. You're as much animal as human, and sometimes the animal is more prominent."

"I don't have a shift." My voice shook.

"But he does. Nick's a nice guy, I guess, but do you think the mountain lion is going to care who it rips through to get to you?"

"We were going to talk tonight." The statement wasn't a complete lie. I did hope to talk to Nicholas tonight.

"Why wait? Put something sexy on. Only that, and I'll let you borrow my trench. And then I'll drive you over to Nick's."

I chewed my lip. "I said talk. I'm not at a point in my life where I'm ready for a long-term relationship, let alone a mate. Besides, I don't own anything sexy. And I don't know where he lives."

Liberty laughed and shook her head. "Do you think mates just pop up out of the blue? You're drawn to each other, like two magnets. You came to Havenwood Falls, which means, whether you consciously think you're ready or not, subconsciously, you were always heading in his direction anyway."

"Are you a shifter?"

"I'm an equal opportunist. And I've been around a while. You don't live in close quarters with a species without getting to know them. But a direct answer would be I went to school with shifters. I've dated a few, and I've buried a few." Her voice grew somber. "Life is short for most. I know it better than a lot of other supes. Take what fate has given you with both hands, Audrey. You won't get a second chance."

Something about the way she said it struck a chord in me. "You were mated to one, weren't you? And you buried him."

Liberty stood up. "Every woman has something sexy. And it's a small town. Someone is bound to know how to find Nicholas. I'll do some research while you're finishing up."

"What if I don't want him as a mate?" The words popped out before I could consider them, and I watched Liberty stop in her tracks and face the shower.

Liberty crossed her arms. "After everything I said, really? I'll humor you. Why do you even think that's an option?"

"I—" I didn't have an answer. All my life I'd been treated like an experiment by other shifters, or a freak by humans when I tried to blend in—and failed. I was never once given a chance to be normal—as normal as a shifter could be—by anyone.

"Listen, I'm going to go dig up an address. You think about it, and we'll talk some more when you're done." Liberty closed the door behind her, leaving me with my jumbled thoughts.

Three days summed up the total time I'd spent so far in Havenwood Falls. I wasn't sure why everyone expected me to make life-altering decisions in such a short amount of time. While I did travel a lot, I was more cautious than impulsive in my day-to-day actions. If I didn't come to terms sooner rather than later, Nicholas would pay the price for my hesitation.

I closed my eyes and lifted my face to the spray of water. The steady shower stream washed away the silent tears. My old life didn't belong in Havenwood Falls. There was really only one choice. I didn't have to like it, but it was the right thing to do.

I snapped off the water and reached for my towel. After wrapping up, I went in search of Liberty and found her on a laptop in her room. "Did you find an address?"

Liberty glanced up from the screen and smiled. "You'll need to get gussied up first. Let's find you something sexy to wear."

~

NICHOLAS

THE DRIVE HOME was usually the time I used to unwind from my day, and began to relax. When I pulled into the driveway, I sat for a while in the truck and studied the cabin of my ancestors. Never had it looked or felt empty before.

I climbed the stairs to my porch. My body ached, not from the hour at the gym or the five-mile run afterward. The tension and pain from my denied mate made my joints feel a hundred years old, not thirty.

My cat was beyond restless, but I didn't want to risk a shift. Giving the cat control, without being completely mated, wasn't a good idea anymore. This morning had been torturous, shifting back. I might not regain control if I tried that again. I scoffed at myself. That would be a perfect way to freak out Audrey.

Something was off. I paused with my hand on the door knob. My cat stood at attention.

The lack of mating was really messing with my head. I smelled Audrey, or at least thought I did. She wouldn't be out here, and she didn't know where I lived to come find me in a cabin in the woods.

I stepped into my home and stood silently in the doorway. No unnatural sounds came to my ears, but the furnace ran, creating enough noise to hide anything quieter. I closed the door and locked it. If someone tried to run, they wouldn't find the door as easily opened as when they entered.

The trench coat folded over the banister gave me pause. I fingered the material, and a familiar, feminine perfume rose. I closed my eyes and took a deep breath. Every muscle tensed, and the fatigue dropped away like icicles in the hot sun.

She was here. In my house.

I took the stairs two at a time. The master suite took up the entire loft area. The potency of her scent strengthened as I approached the sliding barn doors with butterflies in my stomach. When I caught sight of her, my legs froze, unable to move forward or run away.

Audrey sat on the edge of my bed wearing white thigh-high stockings, hooker heels to match, and nothing else. She locked eyes with me and with a saucy smile, leaned back on one arm, giving me an uncensored view of perky tits with nipples begging to be sucked on. Her other hand was busy playing between her spread legs.

"Do you know the problem with being mates with a stranger?" Her husky tone snapped me out of my stupor.

I couldn't find my voice, so I shook my head, my eyes never leaving the hand between her legs.

"That's just it. We're strangers. We know nothing about each other." Her head tipped, and her eyes closed.

"Audrey." My voice was rough, needy.

Her eyes snapped open, and her coy smile returned. "I'm no quaking virgin, Nicholas. If there's something you want . . ."

She didn't have to tell me twice. My clothes fell to the floor in the short distance between her and the door. I dropped to my knees in between her legs, shoving her hand away and burying my face in her dripping pussy.

Audrey gasped, and her hand fisted in my hair. Her hips flexed, and the long moan she emitted made my dick jump. "Not enough. Not enough."

She jerked on my hair hard enough to pull my face away and slide down the bed into my lap. My hands dropped to her hips, pulling her against me, rubbing all that sweet juice against my cock. She ran kisses over my shoulder and nipped my earlobe when she reached it.

"Fuck me, Nicholas. We can make love later. Fuck me now."

I didn't give her a chance to change her mind. Shifting slightly, I breached her tight cunt and thrust in to the hilt. We both groaned, and her arms came around me, nails digging into my back.

"Fuck, kitten. Fuck." My hands tightened on her hips, holding her still, and I buried my face against her neck, kissing and nipping the sensitive skin. I was closer than I wanted to be to finishing, and after days of denial and waiting, I wanted this to last.

"Nicholas." Audrey nipped at my ear and attempted to move. She whimpered when I held her still. Her nails dug harder into my back, and I could swear they felt like a cat's claws. "Move." She bit down on my ear lobe, all gentleness gone.

My control snapped, and I gave her exactly what she asked for. A hand slid up to cup her breast and toyed with the nipple as I pounded into her. Audrey met me thrust for thrust, whimpering and panting out her pleasure. She wrapped around me like ivy on a pole, her mouth everywhere she could reach at once.

Without warning, she fisted her hand in my hair, yanking my head to the side. "I'm going to . . ."

She didn't finish her sentence. Her body tensed, locking me against her as she reached her orgasm. Her teeth nibbled down my neck and blood rushed in my ears as she bit down with full force just above my collar bone.

I growled as my cock exploded, and bit her shoulder. Marking her, bonding to her, just as she had to me. Whether she knew that or not, her shifter instinct had taken over. We stayed locked together, shuddering through the post-orgasm spasms.

Audrey sighed and went limp in my arms. Her mouth pressed absent kisses to the spot she bit.

I nuzzled her jaw, pressing little kisses to her skin until I reached her mouth and could kiss her fully. I felt amazing, completed in a way I hadn't known was missing. I drew away to stare into her beautiful languid eyes. "We skipped a lot of steps."

Her mouth curved. "I have no complaints."

"Why did you change your mind?" I ran my hand through her tangled hair. I would never get tired of touching her.

Her fingers traced the green man tattoo on my pec and followed the tribal lines down my arm. "I missed this somehow."

"We were busy with other things." I cupped my hands around her butt and lifted us off the floor. She laughed, tightening her legs on my waist, and threw her arms around my neck.

"I feel like a weight's been removed. Like I was carrying an albatross I didn't know about." She stretched under me as I laid us down on the bed, like the cat I knew she was.

I wrapped around her, pulling her onto my chest, debating between a nap and slow lazy sex. She decided for us when she curled around me and pressed a light kiss to my pec. I smiled as her breathing evened out and she dropped into sleep.

As I followed her into dreamland, I realized she never answered my question. Not that it really mattered. She was mine, and I was hers. Anything else could be dealt with as needed.

∾

Audrey

I woke up in an empty bed. The sheets were still warm, so Nicholas couldn't have been out of bed long. My eyes found the clock, and I panicked to see it was almost eight. I had to be at work in an hour.

Something shivered under my skin when I jumped out of bed, and I paused to examine the feeling. My skin felt too tight, like it did when

I sunburned. There was no reason for the feeling, and I brushed it off, intent on finding Nicholas and hightailing it to work.

Two steps away from the bed, pain exploded in my head, and I dropped to my knees on the floor. My mouth opened to scream as pain like I'd never felt before erupted throughout my body and dropped me the rest of the way to the floor. My bones felt like they were shattering into pieces while my muscles ripped and shredded like paper.

"Breathe. Audrey, breathe." Nicholas came into my line of sight as I contorted on the floor. "Don't fight it, kitten. Breathe, let it wash over you."

He rested his hand against my cheek. "Come on, kitten, you can do it. Close your eyes. Don't fight it. Breathe and let go."

Easier said than done. I didn't know what was happening, and the pain brought me close to fainting. I reached out a hand to him, and was surprised to see claws where my fingernails were supposed to be.

"Breathe, Audrey. The first shift is always the hardest."

Shift? He said shift. I was shifting? How? Why now?

I closed my eyes as instructed and tried to "let go." But I didn't know exactly what I was supposed to be letting go of. I focused on my breathing. Maybe if I could reach a meditative state, it would help.

I don't know how long I lay on the floor, but at some point, I passed out. When I came to, Nicholas still sat next to me. I whimpered and tried to crawl over to him.

My movement caught his attention, and he smiled. "There's my pretty kitten. It might take a minute to adjust."

Adjust? I tried to stand and wobbled a moment . . . on four legs. Surprised, I turned and looked at myself, or attempted to.

Nicholas laughed. "Here, there's a full mirror in the walk-in, if you can manage it."

I shuffled and tripped on my own feet as I followed him to the walk-in closet. I huffed and shook my head before pushing back up to my feet and trying again. Was this what a child felt like learning to walk?

My ears twitched, as I could hear all sorts of things now. Nicholas's feet, while nearly silent to anyone else, were easy to discern. The birds nesting in the gutters. It was almost overwhelming, and I bumped his leg with my head.

He pointed to the mirror, and I studied the cougar staring back. The tips of my ears were darker than I remembered for a mountain lion. A different species maybe? What did Nicholas look like as a cat?

My eyes weren't all that different. The pupils had changed, but the golden coloring remained the same. I wondered if Nicholas was a blue-eyed cat. There was no way for me to ask at the moment.

The malachite pendant Addie gave me still rested against my breastbone. If I could shift now, did that mean my curse was broken and she could tattoo me now? The responsible thing to do was to call Addie.

"Okay, kitten. Time for the hard part." Nicholas stepped out of the closet, and I followed, curious as to what he could mean by "the hard part."

He sat on the floor and patted the spot next to him. "You need to shift back."

I balked. My ears lay flat, and I crouched against the floor. Shifting had been so painful the first time. I wasn't ready for that kind of pain again so soon.

Nicholas shook his head. "None of that. You've got to get used to shifting both ways. It gets easier each time. Come on. You can do it laying down as well. Focus on taking control back from the cat. For me, it's a box I put the cat into. Cats love boxes, you know. Set your cat in the box and take back your control."

I rested my weight on the cool wooden floors and did as asked. I didn't think a box would work, but I didn't want to think of it as a cage, either. Instead, I created a cat space in my mind, complete with cute cat tree and play toys.

Coaxing the cat into her play space was harder than I thought it would be. We'd never shifted before, and there was still so much to explore and do. Pain exploded a second time, but briefly, and I found myself shivering with sweat in Nicholas's arms.

"You did fabulous, kitten." He pressed kisses all over my face. "Let's get you washed and fed. Shifting takes a lot of energy."

I did feel weak and exhausted. "I'm supposed to work tonight."

"I've already called Melaina and explained. She didn't sound happy, but it's not like any of us could control your ability to shift." Nicholas picked me up off the floor and carried me into the bath. "We'll go for a run after you eat, and work on your shifting ability." He sat me on the toilet while he ran the water in the jacuzzi tub. "How do you feel?"

"Is it supposed to hurt?" I rubbed my hands up and down my still twinging arms.

Nicholas glanced over at me. "Shifters are stronger than humans for a reason. Yes, it does hurt, but the stronger your muscles are, the less painful the shift. I don't know why that is, probably has something to do with the way our bodies rearrange themselves for the animal. The shift won't ever truly be painless, but go to the gym, do some weight lifting, and you can lessen the pain."

I sighed. "I've always hated the gym."

He chuckled. "Not uncommon for a woman. Come on. Water's ready."

I stumbled when I stood, but Nicholas moved fast and grabbed my arm to steady me. He climbed into the tub with me, and I raised my brows at him. He only smiled and pressed a kiss to my temple.

"You're beautiful in both forms."

I turned and straddled his lap. "I want to see your cat."

Nicholas purred—not a sound I'd associate with a man, but it was sexy as hell—and pulled me closer. His erection rubbed against my thighs. "After."

I didn't ask him after what. Instead I lifted my hips and teased us both by rubbing the head of his cock against my entrance. His hands found my breasts and pinched my nipples.

"Tease." He groaned as I sank down only far enough to take the head of him in.

"Am I?"

"You're playing with fire, Audrey."

"No." I leaned forward and caught his bottom lip in my teeth. "I'm playing with what belongs to me."

Nicholas groaned as I sank down a little further. "Take what you want."

His words were strained, and I felt his muscles quiver under me. I loved that he fought himself to allow me to be in control, but I was done playing. I dropped down, pulling all of him into my heat. His hips thrust up before he stopped himself.

I ran my tongue over his lips and delighted when he tilted his head and let me have access to his mouth. I was done with teasing. I wanted his release. I wanted him to lose control, and I would have it.

CHAPTER 9

NICHOLAS

The woods around my house were the safest place for Audrey to run for the first time. I owned most of the area around the cabin—thanks to my ancestors—and other shifters were mindful of our territories. For the most part. In comparison to what McCabe, the bears, or any of the wolf packs had, it was a pitifully small slice of the pie, but I had never been dissatisfied with it.

Watching Audrey learn the other side of herself was a treat. She frolicked to and fro, taking in the night. I watched her attempt to catch a field mouse end in failure, but she didn't seem to mind, and I wasn't certain she intended on catching it to begin with. She might have just been playing with it.

If she wasn't so new in her form, I might have initiated more intimate actions as well, but we had time, plenty of it, for my dirty thoughts. I wondered if she would be repulsed by the idea. Shifters could and did have sex in either form, but some were prudes. My kitten, so far, was anything but a prude.

Audrey climbed a tree, and I lost sight and sound of her. She was excellent at stealth and needed very little coaching on the subject. I circled around, trying to figure out where she went. When I came back to the tree she originally climbed, I sat puzzled. Her scent circled around a couple of times, but there was no way I should have lost her so easily.

I heard a twig snap and had a split second to react as Audrey pounced from the trees above. She pinned me with mortifying ease and licked my nose. When she took off running, I followed, fully intending to pay her back. I huffed when she vanished again.

A rabbit's scent caught my attention, and mindful not to scare the animal, I hunted. The smell led me to a small clearing along the creek, where I found Audrey already on the trail. I hung back, waiting to see what she would do about the rabbit. We'd eaten before heading out, and while I could always eat again, I wanted to see if her instincts would allow her to eat the fresh rabbit, or if she'd simply play with it the way she had the mouse.

I didn't have a long wait. Catching her scent, the rabbit took off running down the creek bank. Audrey gave chase, and for the first time, I realized she was wicked fast. Cougars were fast sprinters on the whole, but she took it to another level.

She caught the little animal as it tried to cross the creek and audibly snapped its neck. With what could be called a happy trot, she brought the rabbit to me and dropped it at my feet.

I gave her a lick on the cheek for the successful kill. She pushed the rabbit with a foot toward me and tipped her head. She wanted me to have it.

Shrugging my shoulders, I stretched out and began my little feast. The rabbit was decently fat—no doubt ready for winter. Audrey sat nearby, cleaning between the toes of a front foot, seemingly satisfied with herself.

Without warning, she stood and growled. All the fur on her body stood on end. I paused my chomping and glanced in the direction of her attention. Two wolves stood down the creek a little, close enough to catch our attention but far enough not to be a threat yet. They were announcing themselves, politely, though Audrey didn't know that.

The Kasun wolves didn't often come onto my land without reason, and though Audrey had met the sheriff in person, I doubted she'd recognize him in wolf form. I chuffed at her and walked over to the wolves, sitting a few paces from them.

Ric, the bigger of the two, stomped a foot, and jerked his head toward my cabin. He wanted to talk, but I couldn't fathom why. I nodded to Ric and turned back to Audrey.

She stood over the partially eaten rabbit in a protective stance. I had no doubt if the wolves had tried to take her kill, there would have been a fight. I picked up the rabbit remains and headed toward home. I didn't hear Audrey follow, but I'd already gotten used to the fact I wouldn't hear my woman unless she wanted me to.

I carried the rabbit up to my porch and shifted. Audrey's kill went into the unlit grill to be dealt with later, and I grabbed my pants. As I pulled them on, I noticed the sheriff's black Chevy truck in my driveway. The wolves walked over to the vehicle before shifting, and put their clothes on.

Audrey sat on the other end of the porch and whined a little. I walked over to her with my shirt in hand and sat down next to her. I worried that shifting would always be hard for her. It wasn't a skill that usually had to be acquired as an adult. We learned how to shift from the onset of puberty. She didn't have that luxury.

She shied away as footsteps echoed on the porch. I glanced over at the sheriff and deputy. "Could you give us a minute? There's coffee and cake, if you want to wait inside."

Ric raised his brows and touched Conall's arm before the younger wolf could object. "Sure. You have cream and sugar?"

"Yes. Make yourselves at home." I waited for them to walk away before turning back to Audrey. "Come on, kitten. We have company."

She whined again and moved forward, dropping her head in my lap. Her breathing labored, and I watched her muscles ripple and shift. After what felt like an eternity, my naked mate lay quaking in my lap.

"I've got you." I pulled my shirt on over her head and carried her into the house. I stopped in surprise when I saw Addie sitting in one of the living room chairs.

"What's this about?" I asked no one in particular as I made Audrey comfortable on the couch.

"Best if Addie explains." Ric sipped from the coffee cup he held.

"A few hours ago, a magic bomb, for lack of a better term, exploded inside the wards. The only thing different after the bomb went off, besides the extra magic lingering in the air, is that Audrey's registry went dark." Addie tipped her head at my mate. "We've got a couple of witches collecting the excess before it does any damage, and I'm here to see why Audrey's registry suddenly stopped working when it was fine before the magical incident."

Audrey pulled the malachite necklace off and tossed it to Addie with minimal movement. She looked exhausted. I needed to talk to my parents about her shifting. I didn't want it to be a strain on her every time it happened. I didn't remember it being like that as a teen.

Addie studied the stone, held it up to the light, and cupped it in her hands. "That's so weird. The magic is gone. As if it was never there to begin with." She looked at Audrey. "May I?"

Audrey nodded, and Addie moved to sit next to my mate. I hovered nearby as Addie did nothing more than hold her hand. "The magic surrounding you is gone as well. Whatever curse kept me from registering you is broken somehow."

Audrey's cheeks went pink. "I'm Nicholas's mate. That's the only thing that's changed in the past few hours."

Addie puffed out a breath and sat back. She looked out the window at something none of us could see. "It's possible. I mean, it would be the most ass backwards protection spell I'd ever seen, but I suppose it's possible."

"What are you talking about?" I crossed my arms and stared down at the women.

"Audrey can explain. I'm going to go get my tools out of the sheriff's car. I can officially do her registry tattoo now." Addie stood, and both the sheriff and deputy followed her out.

I sat down in Addie's vacated spot. "So. What am I missing?"

Audrey reached out and linked our fingers together. "I'm not even sure where to start."

I squeezed her fingers. "Let's try the beginning."

She chewed her bottom lip before nodding slowly. There was

nothing she could tell me that would drive me away, but her nervousness came through our linked hands. After a moment she took a deep breath and sighed. "I think I was born in Virginia."

"Think?" I slid closer and pulled her into my lap. "There's nothing you can tell me that will change what is."

Audrey leaned against me and sighed. Her words tumbled out, and with each new fact, my heart hurt a little more. She had drifted from place to place; she had no one to call her own, no place to call home.

"You'll never be alone again, kitten." I placed a kiss on her cheek. "Tomorrow, we'll go get your stuff, and then I'll take you to meet my parents, and see if my sister can bring her son, Finn, over. You have my family now."

"They probably won't approve." Audrey tilted her head up to look at me.

"We're not snobs. Mom will love you. She got another son when Becca mated, and now she gets another daughter." I kissed the tip of her nose. "You have nothing to worry about."

Addie reappeared, carrying her worn bag. "Let's get this show started."

~

AUDREY

MEETING NICHOLAS's family wasn't as terrifying as mating with him. I played the scene at breakfast over again in my mind as we walked back to the cabin from Creekwood. His parents were loving and accepting—it was clear where Nicholas got it from.

"You're thinking awfully hard, Kitten." Nicholas jumped stones across the creek and waited for me to join him.

"I've never met shifters like your family. Even in the commune, shifters were . . . different." I accepted his offered hand.

"Things are different in Havenwood Falls. The rules are heavily enforced . . ." His voice trailed off.

77

"Have you ever broken the rules?" I didn't think so—Nicholas was a rule follower—but we were still learning each other.

"No. Mike McCabe's son—Braden, my best friend—he broke the rules to protect his sisters. He died, and the girls were banned from Havenwood Falls." Anger clipped his words.

"You don't agree with the ban?" I squeezed his hand, and he responded in kind.

Nicholas sighed. "The rules exist to keep us all safe. There are no exceptions, though I think the witches bend the rules as far as they can sometimes, and the fae think they're more guidelines than rules."

We exited the trees and walked into the yard. Nicholas turned and pulled me into his arms. I laughed as he rubbed his nose over my face and his fingers teased my sides.

"You want to go for a run?" He followed his nuzzling with kisses. "I think you can manage the lower trails up the side of the mountains."

He tensed suddenly and released me. Nicholas stepped around me to stand in front as two large wolves moved out of hiding in the trees. Both growled low, and their hackles stood tall on their backs. Hostile, and a clear threat.

Nicholas held his voice low as he took two steps forward. "Run, Audrey. Go back to my parents."

I couldn't move. Something about the wolves felt familiar, though I couldn't place why. They were shifters by their scent, and something about their smell nagged at memories that didn't exist.

"Run, Audrey!" Nicholas shifted as he lunged forward, and the first wolf moved to attack. His shout startled me into motion, and I pivoted, running full speed into the trees.

I couldn't shift as fast as Nicholas. My shift took time and meditation. All I could do was hope I could outrun whoever followed on my two legs. I didn't turn to look when leaves crunched behind as fast as they crunched under my own feet.

Something plowed into me as I jumped the creek. The water was frigid, but I barely felt it over the panic that seized my mind. I scrambled to my hands and knees as a cougar sailed over my head.

I pushed to my feet and ran for the trees. I grabbed a low hanging branch, and ignoring the rough wood, pulled myself up. I continued up until I found a secure spot to wedge myself in. It was all I could do without my shift.

Tears ran down my face as I tried to process what was going on. There was an angry bear below, which for reasons I didn't know, was fighting a cougar I didn't recognize by scent, and Nicholas fought two other wolves I was sure didn't belong in Havenwood Falls.

A cougar screamed, and I watched as a second one jumped down from a tree onto the bear's back. The two cats moved with a synchronicity that spoke of long-time familiarity. The bear made the cats look small, but they were faster.

Fear beat in my ears. I didn't know what was going on. Without knowing whom to trust, there was nothing I could do. I was useless.

The bear reared back, throwing off the cougar on his back. He went flying and struck a tree hard. However, the motion left an opening for the other cat to lunge and latch onto the bear's throat. The bear came down on the cat, but he didn't let go of his choke hold. Despite the wild thrashing, the cougar remained stubborn, and the bear slowed and dropped.

The second cougar shook himself and came over to my tree. He sat and waited while the other cat retained his chokehold. When it was clear the bear wasn't getting back up, the cougar released the bear's throat and limped over to the tree.

I leaned forward to get a better look as the cougar limped over to where his partner sat. Angry red furless scarring covered a shoulder, down a front leg and part of his torso. He flopped down, and I could feel his fatigue in the motion. The uninjured cat began bathing his partner. They seemed unthreatening and in no hurry to move along.

Where was Nicholas? Should I trust these cats? Were they shifters? Based on behavior alone, they certainly didn't act like wild animals, and they lounged at the bottom of my tree, waiting me out. I couldn't stay up here forever. Despite my better judgment, I slowly climbed down the tree.

The cougars stretched and rolled over to expose their bellies to me.

I realized one was a male and the other—the scarred one—was a female. Confused, I wrapped my arms around myself. "I don't know what that means."

The scarred cat rolled to her feet and bumped my legs. My hand automatically went out, and she licked it. The male rolled back up and sniffed my hand before licking it as well.

"Okay. I get it. You're friendly." I looked toward the cabin. Was Nicholas okay?

The female walked a few paces off in the direction of the cabin, and then stopped. She looked back at me. Her partner joined her and sat.

"There were wolves. Nicholas . . . he tried to stop them while I ran." I wasn't proud of the admission, but there was no way I could have helped him.

The female stretched and yawned before moving a few more feet toward the cabin and waiting. My plan was to wait for Nicholas to find me. I glanced back at the unmoving bear. If they could bring down a bear, there wasn't really anything to be afraid of. Was there?

CHAPTER 10

NICHOLAS

*D*umb fucking dogs. I rolled my shoulders and watched as Conall slammed his cruiser door closed. The car was enhanced to hold supes, so I didn't worry about the trespassers getting out of it. I turned my attention to the wolves that had saved my ass.

Theo and Iris from the inn. Well, Theo had backed me up while Iris held onto his clothes. She hadn't been happy about that role either. She-wolves, in my mind, were more vicious than males. She'd have likely killed the trespassers by accident.

Sheriff Ric shook his head as Conall climbed into the cruiser and left. "Been chasing those wolves all over town. Like I was some damn bill collector and not the sheriff. I have better damn things to do than play hide and seek with a bunch of hardheads." Ric looked well beyond angry, which was out of character for him. "And there's still two missing unregistered. You see anybody else strange on your land?"

"Can you talk and run? Something took off after Audrey. I sent her toward my parents, but I don't know if she made it." I edged toward the trees.

"We came to talk to Audrey. We'll go with you." Iris stepped up next to me before I could get too far away from them.

Theo finished pulling on his pants. "It's only right we talk to her first."

Ric held up a hand. "No one is going anywhere. I've got to call the Luna Coven. We need to verify your Registry."

"I'm not waiting for the Court to appear to go after Audrey." I glared at Ric. "I'm not willing to risk a dead mate because you want to be official at a time like this."

"There's Audrey." Iris took two steps forward but stopped and growled.

I turned to see Audrey with two cougars—by size and coloring, juveniles—walking with her. I didn't recognize the cats, but seeing as Audrey was calm, I didn't add that to my list of worry just yet.

"What are they doing here?" Iris crossed her arms.

Theo placed a hand on her shoulder. "They have a right. More than we do."

Instead of commenting on their conversation, I opened my truck to pull out some track pants and a tee shirt. I crossed the yard to Audrey and the cougars and held out the clothes. "They're going to need these if we're going to talk about what just happened."

Audrey wrapped herself around me. "Are you okay?"

"I'm fine." I caught her mouth with mine. "No major injuries."

When the juveniles shifted and took the clothes, I put two and two together. The teens shared an uncanny resemblance to Audrey. Their eyes were as golden as hers. Unlike Audrey, they were filthy.

The girl had terrible scarring on her left side, and the boy had fire in his eyes. He reached for his sister's hand—with as close as they looked in age, I'd say they were twins—and she accepted.

"We're Roxanne and Remy MacKinnon." The girl's smile fluttered. "Half siblings to Audrey."

Audrey jolted and spun on a heel. "What?"

Remy lifted his chin. "It's a long story."

I jerked my head over to where Ric, Theo, and Iris waited. "We've got time."

Audrey nodded to the sheriff and tilted her head at Theo and Iris. She continued to stare as she spoke to the sheriff. "There's a dead bear by the creek. These two took him down as he attacked me."

"Probably one of the other fools I'm looking for. Are you two registered?" Ric pinned the kids with his stare.

"Yes, sir." Roxanne tried smiling again. "Two weeks ago."

There was no hesitation in her words, and I didn't doubt them. The timeline didn't add up, but I kept that information to myself. Audrey had only been in town for four days.

Ric looked over at Theo and Iris. "And you?"

Theo pulled up his shirt to show off the mark along his hip. "You can't see Iris's but we got ours at the same time."

"At least some people can still follow a basic fucking rule." Ric was truly pissed. "I'll call a Bishop over to verify the Registry anyway."

My nose wrinkled at the thought of Roman or Ronan in my cabin. "I'd rather poke a sleeping bear."

"Addie's got some Court things she's doing today. Bishop is a valid alternative to verify the Registry." Ric lifted a brow. "Problem?"

I rolled a shoulder. "I prefer Fairchilds to Bishops."

"As public servants, we're not allowed to take sides."

"As a person who obeys the laws without argument, I prefer Fairchilds to Bishops."

Ric chuckled and some of the anger drained from him. "I'll call Addie and see if she's done with her appointments for today. If not, I can see if Elsmed is busy, but Roman was interested in talking to the shifters that were deliberately avoiding the Registry, so he's going to be nearby anyway."

"My cabin isn't big enough for all these people as it is." The excuse was flimsy at best, but I would stick by it. I didn't want Roman's temper touching Audrey in any way.

Ric nodded. "I'm going to go check on the bear. All of you stay in the cabin until I get one of the Court members out here. No exceptions."

"I don't mean to be crass, but do you have something to eat?" Roxanne rolled her good shoulder. "It's been a long two weeks."

"Come on inside. I'm sure we can find something for you." I led the way into the cabin, wondering what in seven hells was happening.

Only last night, Audrey had no family that she knew of. I wasn't sure I'd like what we were about to hear.

~

AUDREY

THEY LOOKED LIKE ME. The thought wouldn't stop circling through my mind. Roxanne and Remy looked like me. We were half siblings. I wasn't sure if I should rejoice that I had family or weep that I'd been left thinking I was alone all these years.

"I don't even know where to start." Remy pulled out a stool for Roxanne at the bar, and another for Iris, before he set himself between the two girls.

"First things first." I pointed at Theo and Iris. "Who are you?"

"Cousins. On your mother's side. Our father is your uncle." Theo grinned. "Dad will be pleased you're doing well."

"Where is he?" I regretted the question when Iris's face fell.

"Short of the long story, there's a territory war going on. He stayed behind. You have wolf half-brothers, too. Dad worried what would happen to them if you weren't brought back to the valley. He plans to smuggle them out of the territory, if things take a turn for the worse."

"Audrey is cougar *and* wolf?" Nicholas turned from the food he pulled out of the fridge. "I didn't think that was possible."

Remy sighed. "From what we were told, there was some voodoo involved in it."

"That's what we were told, too." Theo nodded to Nicholas when he was handed a plate of food.

"The Shenandoah Valley isn't huge," Roxanne said. "Our pride has held control of the territory for a while. When the Drummond wolf pack from Suffolk, Virginia, came requesting asylum, there was an agreement made with the Shenandoah Pride. Our dad, Wyatt, married Audrey's mom, Marian, as part of the established peace, with a voodoo witch's blessing. It was peaceful at first, from all accounts. Everyone got along on the surface, anyway." She gulped down the water set on the bar.

"Theo and I are part of the Drummond Pack," Iris clarified. "But there was another pack—the Endicott pack—that came from Pennsylvania. I guess they were looking to expand. Archibald, Marian's father—ours and Audrey's grandfather—made an under-the-table arrangement with the Endicotts, and a territory war broke out with the pride. From what Dad found out, Granddad never intended on permanently sharing the land with the pride." She propped her elbows on the bar and rested her head on her hands. She looked wiped out.

Remy nodded at her before turning his eyes back to me. "We went to the voodoo witch in Port Royal, Virginia, for help when the wolves attacked our home and killed everyone. She told us to find the place where magic collects but cannot be found on any map. We've been looking for three years."

"The Endicott enforcers caught up to us in Denver. I took a bit of a beating." Roxy tapped her left shoulder.

"Voodoo doesn't work without a sacrifice of some kind." Theo looked over at the twins. "What did you give the voodoo woman?"

Roxanne's face flushed, and she choked on the food she was wolfing down.

Remy patted her back and rubbed small circles. "We always knew someone was going to ask."

Roxanne swallowed but wouldn't look up from her plate. "Innocence. She wanted our innocence for her help."

I stared, trying to find words as my stomach twisted. Witches could do a lot of things without physically touching, and the voodoo witch likely never touched them but still . . . In the end, I could barely manage a whisper. "Why?"

"We agreed. We needed to find you first," Remy shot back.

I held up my hands. "You've found me."

Had it been worth the price, though? That wasn't for me to decide, even as my heart broke for them. They'd made the choice, and there was no undoing it.

Nicholas looked at Theo. "How did you find Havenwood Falls? I saw you at the inn as well. Why didn't you talk to Audrey then?"

"And get in the middle of your weird mating dance?" Iris snorted. "Not likely. We meant to talk to her that day, but after your pheromones choked everyone within ten feet, we thought it was a better idea to wait until you mated. You'd both be easier to talk to when you weren't so high-strung."

"We were in Denver and saw the ski lodge bus. Iris likes to snowboard. We thought a day of rest wouldn't hurt anyone. We took the bus to Havenwood Falls." Theo shook his head. "It was a complete fluke that Audrey was already here."

Nicholas nodded. I could see he had other thoughts on the matter, but he didn't voice them.

Roxy leaned back in her chair and stared at the ceiling. "The pride matriarch wants you. The original symbol of the peace. She doesn't care about Remy or me. She told Remy he couldn't stay in the pride's territory. Because our father died to wolves, his lineage is weak and of no use to the pride. Where would my brother go? He was exiled for something out of his control."

"Roxy." Remy moved his arm to wrap her in a side hug. "They would have exiled me anyway. The pride only keeps so many men within the territory."

"You weren't even given the option to fight for rank." Tears ran down Roxanne's face.

Icy fingers danced up my spine, and I crossed my arms. "I'm not going anywhere. My mate is here. This is his home, and this is where I will stay."

"Endicott is desperate. The alpha underestimated the strength of the pride and their alliances. He doesn't want to lose any more of his pack to the pride." Theo sighed. "That's why Iris and I came looking. We wanted to talk you into coming home before anyone else died. Endicott sent some of the pack to find you as well, and bring you back, willing or not."

"You can't force anyone out of Havenwood Falls who doesn't want to leave," Nicholas said, coming to my side. "We protect our own. The ones who attacked us will likely have their memories erased and be dumped in Denver or Durango. We don't tolerate having our rules broken."

I turned in to him, closing my eyes and taking a deep breath. He was calm, and it calmed me.

I had just found everything I never knew I wanted in Nicholas and his family. I felt as if some force I didn't understand was trying to pull it all away from me. In a few short days, Havenwood Falls had become home, and I wasn't going to give that up without a fight.

The twins had nowhere they could go. In theory, if I returned, they would still be homeless. They were my father's children. Regardless of never having them in my life or me in theirs, they were here now, looking for help. How would I live with myself if I abandoned them the way I was abandoned?

"I am by your side, no matter your decision." Nicholas pressed a kiss to my head.

"Your brothers need you as much as your cougar family does," Iris growled. "Are you going to abandon half your family to death because you don't share their shift?"

"Iris." Theo whomped the back of her head. "That was uncalled for."

"I will not apologize." She clenched her jaw.

"They have my uncle, don't they?" I watched Iris's face darken. "They don't need me. The twins have no one, and my place is here."

Nicholas patted my butt. "I have a few calls to make. Holler if Ric returns before I come back down. Put the twins in the guest room after they're done eating. They could use a shower and some sleep."

"All right." I didn't know what he was up to, but I trusted him, so I didn't ask.

"Why aren't we good enough?" Iris deflated in her seat. "We're family, too."

I considered my words. "No one in Shenandoah wants me for who I am. They want me for what I can do for them. That's no way to live."

Theo sighed. "It really isn't, is it?"

"We should contact Dad. Let him know." Iris looked ready to cry. "We're going to lose everything."

"We'll be alive. And that's always a pretty good starting point." Theo rubbed a hand along the back of his neck. "We should head back to the inn and call Dad."

"Fine." Iris marched to the door and slammed it on her way out. Theo hesitated.

"No one is making you leave Havenwood Falls," I offered quietly.

"Iris is a dreamer at heart. I think she imagined some big reunion with tears and hugs and instant love for family. The rest of us are a little more of realists." Theo's smile didn't touch his eyes.

Her dream made me a little sad. "I don't remember any of you."

"Voodoo witch," Roxanne offered with a yawn. "She took your past for your spell's payment. We asked when we were trying to haggle our own payment. You'll never remember Virginia."

Theo nodded. "That actually fills in some of the blanks."

Roxanne pushed her plate away and laid her head on the bar. "I think I'm ready for that shower and bed."

I nodded. "All right. The guest room is at the end of the hall there. I'll run up and grab some clothes for you guys."

"Thanks, Audrey." A dimple I hadn't noticed appeared on Remy's tired face.

I walked with Theo to the door. Iris was on a cell phone, pacing the porch. Her face was contorted in anger.

Theo turned to me as he stepped out. "We'll likely be here for a while until Dad makes a plan. Havenwood Falls seems the safest place to be for the moment. Thanks for at least talking to us, and not throwing us out. We'll go down to the Police Department and wait on the sheriff there. Iris likely won't be coming back inside to wait."

"You know where I'm at if you need me."

He nodded. "See you around."

I closed the door behind him and watched as he approached Iris. She didn't look any more pleased at whatever he said to her, but together they walked down the drive. Sorrow stung my soul that I couldn't be who they needed me to be, but my place was here. With Nicholas. I shook off the dreary thoughts.

As I ran up the stairs, I hoped Nicholas had some idea what to do about the twins. The cabin was only so big, and they were of an age they shouldn't be sharing a room for any length of time. I wanted to help, but I had no idea where to even start. Scratch that. The starting point would be clean clothes. Everything else would hopefully fall in line.

CHAPTER 11

NICHOLAS

*M*y first call was to Mike McCabe. I wasn't alpha, and to make any form of pride decision without him was terms for him to call me out. I didn't want to be alpha, so avoiding the challenge was important.

"McCabe."

"It's Nicholas. I have a situation. I was wondering if you and Anne would mind coming out to the cabin. And would you mind calling my parents as well? I have another call to make after this one."

"What's going on, Nicholas?"

"It's best to explain everything at once. We have a dilemma, and it's not something Audrey or I can solve without help."

"Audrey?"

Shit. I forgot to introduce them. "My mate. That's another long story."

"Give me the cliff notes, son."

I sighed. "She totaled her car. I was the rescuer. She's my mate."

"All right. I'll bring some meat over. We'll light the grill."

Tension tightened the muscles between my shoulders. "Ask my mother to bring sides, then. I've already fed a houseful of shifters once today, and haven't had the chance to call the butcher."

"I'm going to want to hear this full story when I arrive."

"You'll get it. I promise." I smiled at Audrey as she came into the room and dug around in the closet. When she came out with clothes, I realized I didn't ask the twins where their belongings were. As filthy as they were, I doubted they even had anything. They likely spent most of their time in shifted form—risky, with the hunting season open in Colorado.

"All right. We'll see you in about an hour."

"Good enough." I hung up and wrapped my mate up in my arms when she came out of the closet. "Has Ric come back?"

"Not yet." She leaned in, and I groaned when she nibbled on my lip.

"We don't have time to finish what you start." But I still pulled her down onto my lap, making sure to grind my erection against her on the way down.

"If I didn't know any better, I would call you a horny dog." She wiggled deliberately, rubbing herself against me.

"I'm not the only one." I pressed a hard kiss to her mouth. "Shoo. I have another call to make, and I'm sure the kids would like to cover up and sleep."

"Thank you." She leaned back and cupped her hands around my face.

"For?" I raised a brow.

Audrey grinned. "For being you."

She leaned in and barely brushed her lips over mine before jumping up and taking the clothes down to the kids. That little kitten was going to be the death of me.

The next call was harder than the first to make. I never asked for favors, and favors generally had price tags attached to them.

"Liam speaking."

"It's Jordan."

"I've got my schedule already. I know I'm on call for the next week."

I hesitated.

"What is it?" Liam cut through bullshit faster than I ever could.

"There are some . . . issues . . . surrounding Audrey. This guy,

Endicott, is trying to forcefully take her from Havenwood Falls, as some kind of peace offering for the pride in Shenandoah Valley, Virginia."

"What are you asking for, Jordan?" Simple and straight to the chase. There was no judgment in his voice, or curiosity.

"I know you and Savage have connections around the country. Is there a way to make it clear to both parties that Audrey stays where she's at until she wants to leave?"

Liam snorted. "Your mate isn't going anywhere."

"I know."

There was a pause on the line. "I see."

I waited. There was nothing else for me to say. I asked, and Liam, president of the outlaw motorcycle club SIN, either accepted or denied.

"Those shifters trying to avoid the Registry wouldn't have anything to do with this, would they?"

Asking him how he knew about that was pointless. There was very little the MC didn't know about. "They're part of the problem, yes."

"How's your kitty cat feel about this?"

"I hadn't planned on sharing this with her. I want her happy, not stressed and anxious."

Liam snorted. "That's a bridge you don't want to be on when it's burning." He sighed. "Everything has a price."

"She's worth it."

"Lovesick fool." But Liam laughed again. "Let me do a little digging. I'll have to see if my arms stretch to Virginia, and I'll get back to you. I don't want to hear shit when you're called out to the club in the middle of the night to deal with some trauma."

"Make this problem go away, and I'll be in the clubhouse, whistling a merry tune."

"I'll call you back."

"Looking forward to it." Not really, but what else could I say. Being club bitch for their injuries was a small price to pay for Audrey's safety and happiness.

~

AUDREY

My first impression of Mike McCabe was one of strength. Not only because of his build, but his demeanor as well. He was a man you wanted on your side in a fight. His wife Anne was small in comparison, but there was nothing about her I'd call weak either.

They came in with Nicholas's parents as the sheriff and Addie were leaving. Mike carried what looked like half a dozen of ribs over one shoulder and a bucket of ice cream in his free hand, and the women carried in bowls of side dishes. Nicholas's father, Ronald, stopped the sheriff on the porch for a brief conversation before he came in with several bottles of spirits.

"What's going on?" I pinned Nicholas with a look.

He came over to my side and wrapped an arm around my waist. "Pride meeting. Sort of. Mike is pride leader in Havenwood Falls and you haven't met him yet. And we need to discuss the twins."

As if on cue, the twins came out of the guest room, rumpled but looking more rested. Remy yawned, and Roxanne automatically moved into the kitchen to help Anne and Elaine, Nicholas's mom, with the sides. Remy glanced around and decided on the path of least resistance. He walked over to the couch and stretched out.

"Nicholas, why don't you get the grill lit? These are going to need a few hours." Mike patted the pile of meat with something close to affection.

"I lit it when you said you were coming with a hog." Nicholas waved to the giant grill on the deck. "Go ahead and put that thing in. It'll be done in time for supper, I think."

"Good lad." Mike disappeared outside with his meat, and both Ronald and Nicholas followed.

"This fridge is a disgrace." Elaine's sigh could be heard through the entire first floor.

"We ate it all." Roxanne's soft voice contrasted with the women's.

"Well, at least there's room to put stuff away until it's time to heat it up. Why don't you go sit with your brother, dear? You look a bit dead on your feet." Anne phrased it as a suggestion, but it was clear she expected it to be carried out.

I sat on a chair as Roxanne practically lay on top of her brother on the couch. He shifted enough to let her slide behind him against the back of the couch, and they were both asleep in seconds.

"Aren't they cute?" Anne came out of the kitchen, carrying a drink tray. She studied the sleeping twins. Her eyes narrowed a moment. I watched as she set the tray on the coffee table and reached for Roxanne's left arm.

Remy's hand shot out and grabbed Anne's wrist before she could touch Roxanne. They both froze, and for a moment, I thought she would scold Remy. Anne's face softened, and she patted his hair. "You're safe here. I just want to see how bad the scarring is."

Remy released her hand and ducked his head. "I'm sorry. Caught me by surprise."

Anne ran light fingers down Roxanne's arm, over the scars, before she picked up the young girl's hand. "How long had you been taking turns on alert?"

Remy yawned and scooted farther into the couch. He looked like he was already mostly asleep again, but he answered her. "Couple years. Safer that way in strange territories."

I waited for Anne to finish her examination. "Something wrong with Roxanne's scars?"

"They're deep. Really deep. It's going to limit her mobility. Poor thing. She needs a skilled healer. Jasper may be able to heal the deeper part, leaving the surface scars." Anne poured lemonade as the men came back in from outside. "Lemonade?" She offered Mike the first glass.

"Thank you, dear." He sat in the other vacant chair.

Nicholas, to my surprise, sat at my feet and leaned back against me. I ran my hand through his hair, delighted when he purred.

"Here we are." Elaine came out of the kitchen carrying a cheese-and-fruit tray. "Something to hold us over."

"So. There are obviously a few new things to discuss." Mike gestured to me. "Nicholas is mated. What are your intentions, son?"

"I plan to continue as I have been with Audrey at my side." Nicholas wrapped an arm around my leg and kissed my knee.

"I hoped one day Braden would make the challenge for alpha and let this old man retire. Should I expect your challenge soon?"

Nicholas shook his head. "You'll have to wait for Finn to grow up for that. Unless Ethan wants to take the mantle from you. I'm content."

Mike sighed and sat back in the chair. His weathered face suddenly looked a hundred years old. "You have potential. You always did." His eyes traveled to where the twins snored together. "The kids?"

"My half siblings through my father." I sat up and met his gaze. "They're now orphans."

"I wanted to propose an adoption by the pride." Nicholas sat up. "That would, of course, leave their primary care to you with the rest of the pride filling in as needed."

Mike pursed his lips and looked at his wife. She wore a considering, pensive face. "That's a lot to ask of the pride."

I wanted to protest, but before I could put the words together, Nicholas spoke again.

"As much as I love my mate and want to give her anything she desires, Audrey and I don't have the knowledge or space to take care of growing shifters." Nicholas squeezed my leg. "And Audrey struggles with her own shift."

I twisted his ear, and he yelped. "You could be a little more abstruse about that. I can shift; it just takes time and focus."

"But it shouldn't." Elaine folded her hands together. "Shifting is as natural as breathing. You shouldn't struggle with it."

"I didn't come into it until about twentyish hours ago." I debated boxing his ears when all eyes fell on me. "It's complicated."

"She was cursed to be shiftless until she mated." Nicholas cupped his hand around his ear.

"We can work on it." Elaine's statement made that part of the discussion final, if the nod from Anne was any indication.

Anne waved a hand at the twins. "I don't agree with a pride adoption. It wouldn't sit well with the Court, and if something happens to their caretaker, the children are left floundering within the pride. Mike and I will adopt the children. We'll give them the choice to change their names to McCabe or retain the name of their birth." Anne lifted her chin, almost daring Mike to challenge her decision, but he smiled at her.

"That's sound. They'll have plenty of room in the house, and we certainly know how to handle a teenager or two." Mike nodded. "And of course, Audrey, Nicholas, you're welcome to check in on them, and they're welcome to visit you at any time."

Remy stretched without sitting up. "I think I'm supposed to complain about not being wanted, but that's really not the case, is it?"

Roxanne propped her chin on her brother's shoulder. "It's going to be weird, in a pride where the matriarchy doesn't rule, but I'm game."

"We've got a couple of backpacks of stuff in one of the abandoned mines nearby. Roxy and I can fetch them after dinner."

Anne paled. "One of the mines? They're dangerous."

"So is rolling over in a tree." Remy sat up and continued rolling his shoulders and stretching his muscles.

"We have rules." Mike sent him a pointed look.

Remy reached for the cheese on the tray. "Good parents do. It's the parents without rules you've got to worry about."

Ronald snorted and stood. "Thank you, my friend, for accepting this challenge. I'll get you a beer."

CHAPTER 12

NICHOLAS

I stood next to Audrey on the porch as she hugged and kissed the twins goodbye. She was nervous for them, but they were smart kids, and I didn't think they'd have any problems with the McCabes. In the yard, the twins handed Anne their borrowed clothes and shifted next to the waiting Mike and Ronald. They took off into the trees with the men behind them. They were going to the mine to collect the twins' meager possessions, and the women would meet them at home.

We waved as Mom and Anne backed out of the drive. Call me selfish, but it was nice to finally have my house back to myself—and my mate—after the day we put in.

I wrapped around my mate and pressed kisses to all the bare skin I could reach. "Want to go inside and snuggle?"

Audrey laughed and pulled away. "I have to work tonight."

I groaned. "I make enough for both of us. You could quit, take care of the house. Be a kept woman."

"And pigs could fly." She twisted out of my reach when I grabbed for her. The grin on her face was full of mischief as she darted inside.

"We could snuggle naked before you go to work." I leapt at her, and she danced away, laughing.

"Maybe I don't want to snuggle." She took the stairs two at a time, pulling off her shirt as she went. "I have something more . . . adult in mind."

My cock jumped to attention, and I growled, stalking her up the stairs while weaving around her discarded clothing. "You're playing a dangerous game."

She glanced over her shoulder, naked as a jay in the center of the room. "Fortunately, it's a game we both win. But sadly, you're wearing too many clothes to play."

I grabbed her before she could evade me again and rubbed my erection into her ass. "You are a troublemaker."

She lifted her arms behind her and wrapped them around my neck. "You can't live without me."

"No. I can't." I turned her, rested my forehead against hers, and kissed her again, nibbling a little at the corner of her mouth. "You are every star in the sky, every song on the wind. There's no possible way for me to love you more, and yet I don't think there's any way to measure just how much I do love you."

Audrey's brows rose even as her lips curved. "Who wrote the poetry?"

I nipped her lip, hard. "We belong to each other. You have my mark; I have yours. But it's not enough. I want you to have more than that."

Confusion crinkled her face. "I don't understand, Nicholas."

"You have my heart and soul. I've given you my home. I want to give you something else." I stepped back and pulled a small black box out of my pocket. "I always thought it a pointless human tradition. We're shifters. We have mates or we don't. And yet, the other day I found myself wondering if you would accept being more than just mates. I had planned this to go a different way, but this is as good a time as any. Will you take my name, Audrey? Will you let me give you this last thing I have to give?"

Her mouth fell open. I hadn't opened the box. By the look on her face, I didn't need to.

Audrey leapt up, wrapping arms and legs around me and fusing her mouth to mine. "I'll take everything you wish to give me and give back everything in my power to give you, I promise. I love you."

I carried her over to the bed and pinned her underneath me. I gave her a wicked grin. I ground my quickly hardening cock against her cleft.

Her eyes half closed, and she arched up against me, creating mind-numbing friction. "Tease."

"Should I collect on your promise now, then?"

"I insist." With mischief on her face, Audrey flipped our position so she straddled me.

She leaned back enough to slide her hands under my shirt as she gyrated her hips over my stiff cock. There was a wicked gleam in her eyes when she leaned forward and nipped my bottom lip between her teeth.

Her nails scraped lightly over my stomach and continued up to run over my nipples. She let go of my mouth and dipped back again. "Take the shirt off, or you're going to lose it."

I didn't waste time pulling it over my head. With my eyes on hers, I grabbed the tee by the collar and ripped it down the center for her. Her pupils expanded, and she pounced on my bared flesh.

My hands fisted in her hair when she bit down on my left nipple.

"No." She straightened, linking her hands with mine and pushing them to the headboard. "You don't touch. Let me love on you."

I groaned. "You're going to kill me."

"I have a funny feeling you'll survive." Audrey's hands explored my exposed torso, and where her hands weren't, her mouth seemed to be.

When her tongue dipped under the waistband of my jeans, my dick throbbed, and I twitched in anticipation.

"Audrey." I wasn't sure if I was begging or making a demand, but it didn't matter.

She opened my pants, and I fisted my hands above my head to keep from touching her when her hands closed around my cock. Audrey's purr made my length twitch between her palms, and the little minx tightened her hands as she stroked from base to tip.

Audrey stroked a second time, and I watched her lean down to place a kiss on the tip of my cock as her hands stroked back up.

"Now who's the tease?" I forced the words out as her mouth sealed around the tip of my cock and sucked hard. My hips bucked up of their own volition.

Audrey's mouth was almost as hot and wet as her pussy. The feeling of her gliding up and down, playing with my balls, was almost too much to handle. My hands abandoned their post to tangle in her hair and pull her away from my dick before I exploded.

She chuckled and crawled up my body to give me a kiss. "Something wrong?"

I pulled her in for another kiss, and with my right hand, guided her hips so I could rub my cock all through her wet pussy lips. She groaned into my mouth and shifted enough to allow me to press into her heat. I broke the kiss and rolled us over so I was on top, sinking further into her.

Audrey rolled her hips. Pleasure flickered across her face. "Fuck me, Nicholas."

How was a man to resist the demands of his beautiful mate? I would make sure she never questioned being my mate. For the rest of my life.

CHAPTER 13

AUDREY

Coffee Haven bustled with activity. I stirred my coffee, waiting. Apprehension twisted my stomach into knots as I considered how this morning could go. Theo and Iris asked me to meet. I was so anxious about the conversation, I hadn't slept yet.

Iris plopped into the chair across from me while Theo set down a couple of muffins and their coffees. Iris's eyes were puffy, and while I didn't know her well, I knew enough not to ask her about her crying jag.

Theo sat between us, his appearance no less worn than Iris's. He at least attempted a smile in my direction before staring into his coffee. The air felt too heavy to breathe.

"I'm sorry." The words left my mouth before I could consider them.

Iris sighed and picked up her coffee. "You don't have any reason to be sorry. You made the best choice for you." She sounded like she parroted words.

I cupped my icy hands around the warm coffee cup. "What's the plan now? Can I ask?"

"I've gone to the sheriff to ask what would have to be done to become residents of Havenwood Falls, since he seemed like the best source of knowledge. At Dad's request." Theo cut his muffin in half and then in quarters. He picked up a wedge and dipped it into his coffee before taking a bite.

"He's got Milo and Felix, your brothers. They were in Illinois when we spoke. Some place called Peoria. He's taking precautions as they head this way." Iris stole a piece of Theo's muffin and ate it in one bite, without dipping it into the coffee.

My heart fluttered. "You want to stay?"

"There's nothing left in Virginia. Without you, the pack and the pride are in an all-out war, and it's not the best place for any kind of shifter to be at the moment, as it will require declaring loyalty to one or the other." Theo sliced up the second muffin.

Iris propped her elbow on the table and rested her chin in her hand. "I do like it here. The slopes are killer. I homeschooled in Virginia, since I was ahead of my class in nearly everything. I don't know if I can continue that here."

I rolled over the information in my mind. My fingers tapped against my cup as I calculated the options. "I can't make any promises—I'm new here, too—but I can talk to Nicholas and his parents. They're not huge, prominent figures in Havenwood Falls, from what I've seen, but their family's been here for generations. I think we might be able to work it out for you all to stay."

"We appreciate any help you want to offer. Dad won't be in the area for about another week. We wanted to make sure we had everything in order for when he got here." Theo pushed the muffin plate toward Iris.

"What do you plan on doing in Havenwood Falls?" I sipped from my cup.

Iris shrugged. "Live, I guess. Go to school, flirt with boys. See if I can get a job on the slopes."

Theo rolled his eyes. "You're too young for a job. Let's not let Dad hear you talk about flirting with boys. Dad's a surgeon. I haven't checked out the employment offerings yet, to see if Dad could find work in a town this small."

"A surgeon?" I tipped my head.

Iris nodded. "Trauma surgeon. He started his residency as an ER doctor, but after a couple of years, redirected to trauma surgery. I never asked why."

"I haven't either." Theo shrugged. "Just a calling, likely. Dad does stuff on impulse a lot of the time. Remember when he thought it was a good idea to breed rabbits?"

The thought didn't process. "Rabbits? But you're . . ."

Iris snorted. "We know. The plus side? We didn't have to go very far for fresh meat that winter."

I shook my head. "But why?"

Theo shrugged. "Who knows?"

Talking about the past brought up a question I hadn't really considered before. "The twins said the pack killed our dad, but what happened to my mom?"

Both Theo and Iris sobered.

Theo ran a hand through his hair. "She died. A couple of months after Granddad's announcement to support Endicott. She seemed a little crazed, and I think it might have been the voodoo witch's blessing turning in or something."

"Oh." I didn't know what else to say.

"Did you want to come house hunting with us?" Iris gestured out the window. "We originally thought the apartments looked nice. But they're not really big enough for all of us."

Before I could answer, Theo held up a hand. "No pressure. You can tell us no."

Iris sniffed. "You can even bring along the twins. Since we're all family in some kind of way, it's only logical we try to get to know each other before we settle on mutual distaste."

"I can see what the plan is with the twins. Maybe we can try to have dinner or something." I didn't think either family would mind sharing a meal. The white elk that the twins, Mike, and Ronald caught on their jaunt to the mines was certainly large enough to feed us all.

The situation couldn't get any more awkward. How did I explain I had wolf shifters and cougar shifters as blood-related family to others? Nicholas didn't care, but he was the best example of open-mindedness not prejudices.

"Great. You should get home and sleep. You look a little dead." Iris stood. "And I want to hit the slopes before Dad cuts me off."

"We can walk with you if you like." Theo copied his sister.

I shook my head. "I'm going to text Nicholas. He'll come pick me up. He dropped me off on the way in to the station."

"All right. We're still at the inn. You're welcome to come talk to us anytime." Theo pointed to the muffin remaining. "Eat that."

I watched them disappear up the block before texting Nicholas. All my life I'd lived as a nomad, never daring to dream for more than an escape from my present. For the first time since waking up memory-less in a hospital in Virginia, I looked forward to my future. I still had no memories of my childhood, but I didn't need them to enjoy today or my new family.

〜

We hope you enjoyed this story in the Havenwood Falls series featuring a variety of supernatural creatures. The series is a collaborative effort by multiple authors.

Havenwood Falls Books by Victoria Escobar:
Shift of Fate
Sun & Moon Academy Book One: Fall Semester

Books in the Havenwood Falls Sin & Silk Series:
Taming the Beast by Nadirah Foxx
Plans Laid Bare by JD Nelson
Shift of Fate by Victoria Escobar
Stolen Wishes by Victoria Flynn
Damned Allure by Justine Winter
Savage Salvation by Kristie Cook
Dark Seduction by Michele G. Miller & R.K. Ryals
Soul Laid Bare by JD Nelson
Stray With Me by E.J. Fechenda
Chase the Flames by Desiree Lafawn

Flirting With Death by Nadirah Foxx

Also try the signature line, Havenwood Falls, the historical paranormal line, Legends of Havenwood Falls, and stories from the local supernatural college in Sun & Moon Academy.

Stay up to date at www.HavenwoodFalls.com

Subscribe to our reader group and receive free stories and more!

ABOUT THE AUTHOR

ONCE UPON A time, long, long ago, Victoria was born in sunny Florida, except it wasn't sunny; it was the middle of the night. Midnight actually, well, two minutes past, but she tried really hard for midnight.

Victoria has attended twenty-one schools in her lifetime. With all the continual switching around, she's relied on her imagination for friends and books for close companions. In high school she remained apart from the crowd and spent most of her time in the library, either reading or writing.

Currently, Victoria has set down roots in New York with her family. She still reads and writes every day. She finished her debut novel *Of Gaea* in the spring of 2013, its sequel *Of Sparta* in the winter of 2014, and has many other projects planned. Look forward to seeing more.

Social Media:

Facebook: facebook.com/V.Escobar.Writes
    Website: vesccobarwrites.com
    Tumblr: authorvescobar.tumblr.com
    Pinterest: pinterest.com/vescobarwrites/

ACKNOWLEDGMENTS

I hate writing these things. I always forget someone.

Thank you, readers, for enjoying Audrey and Nicholas's story, and of course thank you, EJ, for allowing me the honor of writing Nicholas.

I have to say the Havenwood Falls group is one of the tightest cliques of people I've ever had the privilege of working with, and one of the friendliest. Thanks for letting me into your club and humoring the seven million questions.

Thank you, Kristie, for all your hard work, and making my words legible.

Until next time,

VE

AN EXCERPT

~ A Havenwood Falls Sin & Silk Novella ~

HAVENWOOD FALLS

sin & silk

Stolen Wishes

VICTORIA FLYNN

Stolen Wishes (A Havenwood Falls Sin & Silk Novella) by Victoria Flynn

After being gone for several decades, Gabriel Doyle feels drawn to his former hometown in Colorado. His memories are vague and blurry, but he can't resist the urge to go, especially when the woman in his dreams begins to appear in real life. What he's not so sure about is what he faces on his return—leading the Lilith Nest vampires.

Needing a fresh start, Alina Anand takes a nanny job for a mage family in Havenwood Falls. At first, life is great. She loves her charges and finds the town quaint and welcoming, but everything changes when her employers steal her amulet—and take control of her wish-granting powers. Bound to them by tradition, she has no choice but to serve them.

When their destinies collide, Gabriel and Alina discover a connection that goes beyond their undeniable passion. But to save Alina, Gabriel must decide whether to pick up the dark life of bloodshed and revenge he left behind, or to ask for help from those who demand sacrifice. Nothing in life is free. The star-crossed lovers must fight for what they desire most—to be who they are, love who they want, and escape the bonds of their pasts in a town that forgives little and forgets nothing.

STOLEN WISHES

GABRIEL

Her skin was smooth and flawless like Chinese porcelain, and the way her heart drummed excitedly in her chest when I touched her drove me wild. She was a drug I was hopelessly addicted to.

"I've missed you," she whispered, dropping the sheet she had wrapped around herself.

The scent of her arousal invaded my senses and blurred any clear thoughts. All-consuming, that was what the vixen was to me.

Tugging my shirt over my head and throwing it to the ground, I strode toward my prize. Her nipples were drawn up into tight buds as I crossed the expanse of my hotel suite to her. Oh yes, she wanted me. She rubbed her thighs together as if it could relieve the pressure of her desire.

"You're all I can think about. Even when I'm awake, I feel like I'm just passing the time until you're in my arms again," I confessed.

My nameless beauty closed the gap between us, nipping the tender flesh over my collar bone and sliding down me, sinking to her knees. Her hands worked quickly to free me from my slacks. My cock sprung free and her eyes devoured every inch. Her pink tongue swept over her lips, and her eyes dared me to deny her what she wanted.

"Hungry?" I teased, stepping out of my pants and fisting my throbbing cock.

She nodded slowly, leaning forward until her breath fanned over me, making me damn near lose control on the spot. Her fingers skimmed over my sensitive skin before wrapping around me securely. Her hand slid up and down my length lazily, and I let my eyes fall closed, relishing every second. Her hot, slick tongue traced the thick shaft from the bottom up, and her lips enveloped me as she reached the top.

"Fuck," I groaned, my hips flexing instinctively and driving me deeper into her mouth.

I could feel the muscles of her mouth stretch into a coy smile just before she set about her task, taking me in as deeply as she could. Pressure was growing low in my belly, and every nerve was firing like a Fourth of July display. Picking up the pace, her head bobbed up and down as she pushed me faster toward my peak. Her deft fingers worked furiously between her legs. It was a sight that would drive a lesser man to his knees with need, but she was mine, only mine, to savor.

She repeated the same pattern, taking me in deep and then flicking her succulent tongue over the head of my dick. The woman was driving me wild and playing me like a well-loved instrument. Her free hand snaked down, cupping my balls and dragging her nails over them, bringing me to my tipping point.

"Christ, you need to stop, or I'm going to come," I warned her, holding back and giving her plenty of time to release her hold, but she didn't.

Her devious eyes darted to my own, dancing with mirth as she sucked harder. I was a goner under her skilled touch. Not two minutes later, thick ropes of cum erupted from me, coating her throat as I roared in ecstasy. The vixen swallowed down every drop like she was starved for it, drawing it out until my last spasm faded.

She licked her lips with satisfaction, her heavy-lidded eyes betraying her arousal.

"I want more."

Drained of energy, I crossed to the bed and held my hand out to her. Just before she came close enough, the room faded to black, and she was torn away from me.

My eyes cracked open before I could reach her. The room was dark, but I could tell the sun was beginning to set. It was another dream.

Every day for months, the bronzed goddess had visited me and drawn me into her thrall. Women had thrown themselves at me, yet the nameless woman from my dreams had been all I could think about. Hell, my dick wouldn't even respond to another anymore, not of its own volition anyway. My cock was painfully hard, and my fangs dug into my lower lip with my desire, despite the exotic woman's absence.

I could still see her stunning figure standing before me as vividly as though it had just happened, begging me to come for her. Her sensuous voice called to me, telling me she was waiting for me in Havenwood Falls, and I couldn't live on dreams anymore. I had to know if she was real, no matter what.

GABRIEL

There it was again. The relentless pull to leave. This time was different, though. This time, it whispered a name I'd heard before . . . in my dreams. My recurring vision came back to me. An exotic beauty and somewhere called Havenwood Falls. The name had been repeated until it was all I could think about. When I'd done a search, nothing had shown up. I decided to make some calls. Eventually, I'd been able to narrow it down to the mountains of Colorado. No one could remember the town, nor its location, but I'd been told at least twice that I should check out the majestic mountains of the western state. With the red-eye tickets booked, I gave my thoughts back to the beauty who'd been haunting me. I could still picture her sensual form standing before me in my Paris

117

hotel room, whispering for me to come to her in the mysterious town. She was waiting for me.

In the many nights we'd shared, never had I learned her name. It tormented me incessantly. When I ventured out into the city, it never failed that I'd catch a glimpse of a woman who shared some feature with the woman I'd come to care for—long black hair like a raven's feather, a rich tan, eyes like a smooth cognac. Those women were never her.

I pushed the thoughts away, not wanting to obsess over the identity of the mystery woman more than I already had. Swirling my whiskey around the tumbler, I stood on my suite's balcony overlooking Montmartre.

Paris had grown gray with the late autumn season. Rain drizzled down on the city, and I found I wasn't sad to be leaving. When you lived as long as I had, cities like London, Rome, Paris, and Prague lost their luster.

Home.

It was an odd thought. The closest thing I'd ever had to a home had been with my closest friend and sire, Viktor. He'd settled somewhere in Colorado and started a small empire for himself.

He was gone now, which had been a large part of why I'd stayed away from America as long as I had. Would home still be home if the person who made it special was no longer there? That was still to be seen.

"Lorenzo!" I called out, striding into the parlor and abandoning the balcony overlooking the narrow streets of France.

"What can I do for you, sir?" the small Italian man chirped, appearing almost out of nowhere.

"You may let the staff know we will be departing for America in the coming week. Have you ever been to Colorado, Enzo?" I asked, loosening my tie.

"No, sir. This will be my first trip." His thick Italian accent was barely comprehensible. "I hope you'll let me know what to expect and what I should pack for."

"It's late autumn. The Colorado mountains are cold, damp, and could be snow-covered. Layers, my friend."

"*Grazie*, sir. I will make the necessary arrangements. May I ask why the sudden change in plans? I was under the impression we'd be staying in Paris until the end of January before continuing on to Amsterdam."

Lorenzo was good people and the only person I fully trusted. He was nearly forty and had been in my service since he'd reached adulthood. As a blood servant went, he was top notch, and as a friend, he was one of my closest. His family had served me since Viktor had raised me out of the gutter and turned me into a proper gentleman over three centuries earlier. Blend in, watch, find a weakness, and exploit it—those had been my first lessons. I'd done that when I'd stumbled across Alessio De Luca, Lorenzo's seventh great grandfather. He'd been able to do something I'd thought was lost to me since becoming a vampire: he could make me laugh. Instead of killing the poor bastard, I'd offered him a job. The rest, as they say, was history.

"It's hard to explain. I've always been a nomad. However, there's something different about Colorado. It's the closest thing I've ever had to a home, even more than Ireland," I joked, letting my natural brogue slip back into my words.

"How long?" Enzo asked, concern written in the shallow creases beginning to form from age.

Despite being a few hundred years younger than me, Lorenzo looked older than my frozen twenty-eight years.

"I haven't been home in more than forty years. Not since before Viktor passed," I answered, ignoring the pangs of loss that could still send me reeling, if I let them.

"Understandable, sir. He was a father to you, and that sort of grief is felt for a lifetime," he replied.

He was right. I knew Viktor was gone, but going home without his warm welcome would be difficult. That was the thing about vampires —we'd grieve a loss for centuries, because time no longer mattered. Things were felt on a deeper level because such things are fleeting.

"I suppose you're right, but there are other matters to tackle while on this trip," I answered, and there were.

Being a vampire came with its constraints, like not being able to walk in the daylight, but it also gave those like me ample time to grow a fortune. Unlike some, I'd grown with the times, seeing no point in dwelling on the inventions and ideals of the past. When the internet had come along, I'd invested, knowing that it would somehow change the future of the modern world. Then had come the capability to conduct such investments online, and I never needed to work again. When you've been around longer than the stock market itself, you pick up a thing or two about money, stock trends, and good investments. Having spent the better part of two centuries building a fortune, I was now in a position to make moves and flex my muscles. Everyone, regardless of species, could recognize that money was power, and whoever had the most made the rules of how the rest played the game.

"I'm sorry, Gabriel. I don't follow," Enzo said.

I frowned slightly, realizing I hadn't mentioned the dreams or the side trip.

"I apologize, old friend. Things have been difficult. These dreams I've been having . . . I've never experienced anything like them. Actually, I don't believe I remember ever dreaming until a few months ago."

"Would you like me to search the archives? Perhaps there could be an answer there as to what this means?"

I nodded. "Sure. Thank you, Lorenzo. That would be helpful, though my point was that in these dreams, a voice keeps saying *Havenwood Falls.* I think it's in Colorado, near Viktor's old home. I need to know if there's something to all of this there."

"I understand. I'll make the necessary preparations. In the meantime, you haven't fed in a few days," he stated, undoing the button holding his sleeve together.

"I've already booked our flights, but other transportation will need to be arranged."

Enzo pushed his sleeve up, exposing his arm to me. He sat on the sofa, leaving room for me to join him. A pinch in my gums was all I needed to know my fangs had extended, ready to feed. The tight hold I kept on the monster inside me slipped a little, and I pounced on Lorenzo's offering. My fangs tore through his flesh like a hot knife through butter. His blood was like cinnamon and cloves, spicy and aromatic. I drank until the beast inside me was sated and released before I'd taken too much. Like the professional he was, Enzo produced a small hanky and wiped the crimson smear at the edge of my mouth before wrapping his wound tightly. He rose a little unsteadily, my only indication that I'd gotten a little carried away this time. With a quick bow, Lorenzo turned and exited the room.

Shame coursed through me.

There was a time I wouldn't have felt anything for those I'd fed from. Anyone who was unlucky enough to cross my path was lower than me on the food chain; it was natural. That's what I'd told myself for years. Hell, I'd lived for the hunt. The feeling when life finally left someone and the light faded from their eyes had been a drug to me. Viktor and I had even gone to war on several occasions, making a game of killing our foes in the most imaginative way possible. Grown men had fallen in shreds at my feet. Then one day, all of that changed.

I couldn't put a finger on what had been the turning point for me, but after almost a century of living in a constant bloodbath, I'd found myself wanting more. Viktor was calculating. One always had to be on their toes around him. He'd taught me a lot, yet there no longer seemed to be a point to life without someone to share it with, on a different level. I wanted to watch art be born from a beautiful mind and bright thinkers rise to the famed pages of history. I wanted to experience it all as a free man.

As a mortal, I'd been nothing more than a slave. Despite the practice being considered illegal, I'd been taken after the soldiers slaughtered my mother at the Siege of Galway, when King Charles II's men came to topple Catholicism in Ireland. My father had succumbed to the pox a year earlier, along with my little sister, Mary. In my twenty-eight years as a human, I'd never known what it was to do as I pleased. As a vampire, I was desperate for a taste of freedom.

My change of heart had driven a wedge between Viktor and me, but eventually, he came to understand that I needed more than he could give me. Like a baby bird, I had reached the time to leave the nest and spread my wings. So, I did.

In my arrogance and stubbornness, I'd lost almost thirty years with my sire. He'd been gone more than ten years now, lost to the insanity that came with drinking drug-tainted blood. I couldn't help feeling responsible for it. If I had been there, would things have gone differently for him? I'd spent far too long running away from my past, and it was time to go home. It was time to say my final goodbyes to Viktor Azimov, my father and sire, and it was time to look to the future and the mysteries that Havenwood Falls would offer.

Purchase *Stolen Wishes* wherever books are sold.